THE HIDDEN WORLD OF
Changers

No.1: The Gathering Storm

have
FUN
reading!
Love
Ariv

by H. K. Varian

D0954250

Simon Spotlight

New York London Toronto Sydney New Delhi

SIMON SPOTLIGHT
An imprint of Simon & Schuster Children's Publishing Division
1230 Avenue of the Americas, New York, New York 10020
This Simon Spotlight edition June 2016
Copyright © 2016 by Simon & Schuster, Inc.
Text by Ellie O'Ryan
Illustrations by Tony Foti
All rights reserved, including the right of reproduction in whole or in part in any form.
SIMON SPOTLIGHT and colophon are registered trademarks of Simon & Schuster, Inc.
For information about special discounts for bulk purchases, please contact Simon & Schuster
Special Sales at 1-866-506-1949 or business@simonandschuster.com.
Designed by Nick Sciacca
The text of this book was set in Celestia Antiqua.
Manufactured in the United States of America 0516 OFF
10 9 8 7 6 5 4 3 2 1
ISBN 978-1-4814-6617-2 (hc)
ISBN 978-1-4814-6616-5 (pbk)
ISBN 978-1-4814-6618-9 (eBook)
Library of Congress Catalog Card Number 2015945314

Kitsune

One of the most powerful Changers. From the Far East, this massive fox creature possesses many incredible abilities, including commanding fire and creating illusions.

Its fur is typically red, and its paws are engulfed in flame, though they never burn. Kitsunes can have as many as nine tails, which they collect throughout their lifetime by acquiring knowledge or accomplishing heroic deeds. The more tails a kitsune has, the more powerful it becomes.

Nine-tailed kitsunes possess incredible powers, including the ability to see anything happening anywhere in the world. Upon acquiring its ninth tail, the kitsune's fur turns white.

prologue

A streak of red darted over the sand with soundless steps. Tendrils of smoke unfurled from the tracks the creature left behind. With every stride the *kitsune* took, the mist around it thickened— Or was it the smoke from its paws? Or was it something else entirely?

The *kitsune* was quick, but its wits were quicker. There was something in the shadows creeping toward it; something fueled by hatred, by revenge—something so powerful that it threatened the entire world. But the *kitsune*'s allies were near; it could feel them: the jaguar's muscles rippling under dense, silky fur; the thundering wings of the lightning bird overhead. And somewhere beyond the white-capped waves, the seal had command of the sea and all that dwelled within it. The *kitsune* could feel other forces, too; forces for evil that approached with grim steadiness. It was not a fair fight; four against hundreds—thousands—maybe more.

The call of the horn came again, but the *kitsune* did not stop. Its destiny waited in the eye of the storm, and no force in the world could keep the *kistune* from it.

The sky darkened as a sudden burst of thunder crackled overhead.

The *kitsune* pressed on.

Chapter 1
A TIME OF CHANGE

Beeeep. Beeeep. Beeeep.

That sound . . . It was so familiar. . . .

Mack Kimura struggled to wake up, but the dream wouldn't loosen its grip. In the battle between dreams and alarm clocks, though, alarm clocks would always win.

Mack opened his eyes, and the beach vanished, the mist melted into nothingness, and the dark shadow receded. All that remained was the horn. But no, even that wasn't real; it was just Mack's alarm clock. Somehow his dreaming brain must have made it sound deeper.

What a weird dream, he thought, trying to remember exactly what had happened. *Was I, like, some kind of fox?*

But the dream was already slipping away, just like the mist that often rolled over the small coastal town of Willow Cove, where Mack lived.

I've been watching way too many animal documentaries, Mack thought, shaking his head. Mack's grandfather, Akira, was really strict about television. The only shows he ever wanted to watch were nature documentaries. They could be pretty interesting, but Mack would rather watch a superhero movie any day. Their nightly arguments over the remote control were just one of the many ways in which Mack and his grandfather clashed. Sometimes Mack found it hard to believe they were even related.

Mack smacked at his alarm halfheartedly until it finally stopped beeping. Hearing the alarm blaring on a hot, sunny morning could mean only one thing: the first day of school was here. Mack had been counting down for days. It's not that he loved school—he'd rather have summer vacation last all year—but the first day of school meant that his best friend, Joel Hastings, was finally home from his grandparents' farm upstate, where he'd spent the summer. Mack had missed him a ton.

After Mack got dressed, he slung his backpack over his shoulder and ambled down the hall to the kitchen, where breakfast was waiting for him: a bowl of steaming white rice, a banana, a rolled-up omelet, and a saucer of silvery sardines.

"Big day, Makoto," Mack's grandfather said, his wrinkled face grinning. "Sit. Eat."

Mack sat down and reached for his chopsticks. "It's Mack, remember?" he asked.

His grandfather gazed at him with eyes that were the color of the ocean on a stormy day. "You can be Mack if you choose," he said evenly. "I will choose to be Jiji. Or Jiichan, if you prefer."

"Okay, Jiichan," Mack said, stifling a sigh. *Jiichan* was the Japanese word for "grandfather"—it was affectionate, but not quite so affectionate as "Jiji," which was practically baby talk. One thing was for sure, though: Mack's Japanese pronunciation was perfect; Jiichan had made sure of that.

Mack poked at his eggs, wishing that his grandfather could just understand. They didn't live in Japan; in fact, Mack had never even visited the country where his parents had been born. But Jiichan seemed determined to live like he was still there, even though he'd been in the United States for almost seven years now, ever since Mack's parents had died in a car accident when he was five years old. It was the weirdest thing: the longer Jiichan was in the United States, the more ferociously he clung to his Japanese heritage. From the silk screens in the house to the perfectly maintained lotus pond and gingko trees in the backyard, everything felt Japanese to Mack—except himself.

Mack picked up his chopsticks and brought a few grains of rice to his mouth. The eggs and banana would be fine, but there was no way he was going to eat even one bite of the sardines. The last thing Mack wanted was to smell like an aquarium on the first day of seventh grade.

As usual, Jiichan seemed to know what Mack was thinking. He pointed at the shimmery fish with his chopsticks. "Brain food," he said.

"I'm, uh, full," Mack replied.

"More for me, then," Jiichan said as he pulled the porcelain dish across the table.

"You'll be the smartest grandfather on the block,"

Mack joked. He was glad to see Jiichan smile in response.

Mack could just barely hear the rumble of the bus as it traveled toward his house. He grabbed the banana and stood up so suddenly that his chair scraped across the floor. Jiichan winced, but his eyes never left Mack's face.

"The bus," Mack explained as he reached for his backpack.

Jiichan nodded, but there was an expression on his face that Mack couldn't quite figure out. "Yes," he said. "I heard it too. Have a good day at school, Makoto. . . . Mack."

"Thanks, Jiichan," Mack said. He opened the screen door and bounded down the front steps two at a time. When the bus stopped in front of his house, Mack saw that Joel had already snagged their favorite seat—right side, seventh row.

"Makoto, my man!" Joel bellowed as Mack got on the bus. He thrust his hand into the air. High slap, low slap, behind-the-back slap.

Then Mack elbowed Joel and said, "It's Mack, remember?"

"Right. Sorry about that," replied Joel. He scrunched

up his nose to adjust his glasses. "It's gonna be hard to remember. Makoto is such a cool name, dude. Why would you ever want to change it?"

Mack shrugged. How could he explain to Joel, whose family had lived in Willow Cove for six generations? Joel, who always fit in so easily? This year, Mack finally decided he was done with being known as the Japanese kid with the weird name. Starting in seventh grade, he was going to be Mack.

Mack reached into his backpack and pulled out the envelope he'd received a whole week ago. It was still sealed, in perfect condition.

"I can't believe you waited," Joel said, a note of awe in his voice. "I mean, I only had mine for ten hours, and it's been torture."

"You didn't open it, though, did you?" asked Mack.

"Of course not," Joel replied. "You think I'm going to mess with tradition and jinx us?"

Mack grinned at him. Ever since first grade, he and Joel had been best friends—and ever since then, they'd been in the exact same class. Last year, when they moved up to middle school, Mack was sure their lucky streak would come to an end. But somehow, Mack and Joel had beaten the odds and were in all the same classes together.

Would their luck hold out for seventh grade?

"You ready?" Joel asked. "One . . . two . . . three!"

At the same time, the boys ripped open their envelopes. Mack's eyes darted back and forth as he read his schedule. First period, English. Second period, geometry. Third period, earth sciences. Fourth period, band. Amazingly, Mack's and Joel's schedules were a perfect match—so far.

"I've got social studies for fifth period," Joel said. "Then lunch."

Mack nodded. "Me too."

"Seventh period, gym," Joel continued. "You too, right?"

Mack stared at his schedule. The words were clearly printed there: Independent Study: Physical Education. The hint of a frown crossed his face.

Mack's silence told Joel everything he needed to know. "Oh, no," he groaned. "Seriously?"

"I—I don't know," replied Mack. "What's an independent study?"

Joel grabbed Mack's schedule. "Dude, what is this? Some kind of experimental gym class or something? And who's 'D. Therian'? I thought Coach Connors taught all the seventh-grade gym classes."

"A new teacher?" Mack guessed. The name sounded familiar, but Mack didn't remember a Coach Therian from last year.

"I can't believe our perfect streak ended over gym class," he said. "That's weak."

But Mack wasn't ready to accept it. "Maybe it's a mistake," he said. "I've never even heard of independent study classes at school. There's just, you know, *gym*. This has to be a mistake."

Joel looked doubtful. "I don't know," he replied. "That would be a much bigger mistake than a typo or spelling somebody's name wrong."

"It could happen," Mack protested. He twisted around in his seat to talk to Eddie and Miles, who were sitting in the row behind him. "Guys, what do you have for seventh period?" he asked.

"Gym," Eddie replied. Beside him, Miles nodded.

Mack leaned across the aisle to ask Juliet and Maya

and then Ethan and Reese. All of them had seventh- or third-period gym with Coach Connors. Soon, the entire bus was talking about Mack's unusual gym class.

"I'm sorry, buddy," Joel said, shaking his head.

"What for?" Mack asked, sounding more confident than he felt. "Now I know it's a mistake."

Joel raised an eyebrow.

"I mean, come on. If it was an actual class, there would be somebody else on this bus who's in it," Mack pressed on. "When we get to school, I'll go to the main office and ask them to fix it."

"It's worth a try, I guess," said Joel.

Mack glanced down at his schedule again. Those words—"Independent Study: Physical Education, D. Therian, Ancillary Gym"—were all he could see. The longer he thought about it, the less sense it made. Nobody even used the ancillary gym anymore—not since the larger gym had been built a decade ago. In fact, everybody kept saying that school was going to renovate the ancillary gym and turn it into a greenhouse for a new gardening elective. So why would Mack have a class scheduled there? And he had never even heard of a teacher at Willow Cove Middle School named Therian.

D. *Therian*, Mack thought, squinting at the schedule. Dorina Therian!

No wonder he knew that name: Dorina Therian was one of Jiichan's mah-jongg buddies. Every Thursday night, Jiichan and his three best friends gathered around the kitchen table to play mah-jongg. Mack loved his grandfather's game nights—for him, they meant pizza for dinner and complete control over the TV. Mack had known Ms. Therian since he was a little boy. In fact, he'd seen her just four days ago at Jiichan's most recent mah-jongg party. She'd given Mack a lemon square and pinched his cheek as she told him to run off and play, like he was still five years old. With her tiny frame and deeply wrinkled face, Ms. Therian seemed like the last person in the world who'd be teaching a gym class. And wouldn't she have mentioned something to Mack about starting a new job at his school?

A sudden punch to his shoulder jolted Mack from his thoughts.

"Wake up! We're here," Joel said.

Mack shook his head, realizing that half the kids had already filed off the bus. Mack would have to hurry if he wanted to get his gym class changed without being late for homeroom. He couldn't imagine that Jiichan would be pleased if Mack got a tardy on the very first day—that was one lecture Mack would do just about anything to miss.

"Catch you in homeroom, buddy," Mack said to Joel as they were swept into the stream of kids entering the school. Joel flashed him a thumbs-up and continued down the hall toward his locker while Mack turned left toward the main office. *I hope there's not a big crowd today,* Mack thought.

Mack was in luck. The only other person in the office was Mrs. Logan, the secretary. She smiled at Mack over her glasses. "Good morning, Makoto. What can I do for you?"

Mack reached into his back pocket for his schedule, which had gotten pretty crumpled from being passed around on the bus. "It's about my schedule," he said as he tried to smooth it out on the counter. "I need to switch my seventh-period class."

"I'm sorry, Makoto," Mrs. Logan replied, not even

glancing at the schedule. "Switching classes isn't allowed."

The disappointment hit Mack harder than he expected.

"But," he began again, and then swallowed hard. For once, the manners Jiichan had drilled into him over the years were about to come in handy.

"I understand, Mrs. Logan," Mack said politely. "It's just that I think there might be a mistake. I don't even know what 'Independent Study: Physical Education' is, and all my other friends have regular gym with Coach Connors—"

Mrs. Logan was already shaking her head. "We can't bend the rules," she explained. "If we let you switch a class, then we'd have to let the next person who asks also switch a class, and then everybody would want to custom design his or her schedule. It would be a logistical nightmare."

"But why was I assigned to independent study?" Mack asked. "I didn't sign up for it. No one else I talked to is in it—"

"I am," a new voice spoke up.

Mack turned to see Fiona Murphy standing behind him. "You're in independent study for phys ed too?" he asked in surprise.

"Yeah," Fiona replied.

Mack turned back to Mrs. Logan. "Fiona, me ... Who else is in this class?" he asked.

She eyed him over the top of her computer screen. "Well ...," Mrs. Logan began. "I'm really not supposed to share information like that. But since you'll be finding out during seventh period, anyway ..."

Mrs. Logan typed quickly and then peered at the screen. "'Seventh-period Independent Study: Physical Education,'" she read. "'Makoto Kimura, Fiona Murphy, Gabriella Rivera, and Darren Smith.'"

Mack's eyebrows shot up. He couldn't think of a single thing he had in common with Fiona, Gabriella, and Darren. Fiona was supersmart—like, *scary* smart—and took all accelerated classes. As for Gabriella, everyone in Willow Cove figured she'd make it to the Olympics before she graduated from high school. She was that good at soccer—and that determined to succeed, too. And Darren? He was popular with everyone, not because he wore the coolest clothes or anything like that, but because he was honestly, genuinely nice. Darren always waved and smiled at Mack in the halls, even though they barely knew each other.

"That's got to be the most random group of kids at Willow Cove Middle School," Mack said.

Mrs. Logan fixed him with an indulgent smile. "That's because it is," she replied. "Physical education class assignments are generated by the computer. I just print out the schedules."

"But one class for only four students?" Fiona spoke up. "Wouldn't it be easier to assign us to the other gym classes?"

Mrs. Logan's expression didn't change, but her smile looked strained. "The vice principal sets up the classes. The computer schedules the students. I then print and mail out the schedules," she explained, reciting the words as if she'd said them a thousand times before. "What brings you to the main office today, Fiona? I suppose you're also here to request a switch?"

Fiona shook her head. "Actually, it's my locker," she explained. "It's stuck."

"Oh," said Mrs. Logan, sounding relieved. "That's something I can handle. What number is it? I'll send the janitor to take a look."

"Five oh seven," Fiona replied.

Mrs. Logan dutifully wrote it down on a memo pad. "Now, off you two go, or you'll be late for homeroom," she said kindly but firmly, and Mack knew there was no point in saying one more word about Independent Study: Physical Education.

"Thanks," Mack and Fiona said at the same time. They glanced at each other and grinned. Mack reached the door to the office first and pulled it open.

"Do you have Mr. Morrison for homeroom too?" Mack said as they hurried into the hallway. Some kids were still hanging out by their lockers, but the crowd had thinned out. Mack wasn't the only one who didn't want to get a tardy on the first day of school.

Fiona nodded in response. "He's not so bad," she said. "I heard Mrs. Williams gives tardies if anybody is even *talking* when the first bell rings."

Mack groaned, shaking his head.

Just then, someone pushed past Fiona.

"Hey!" Mack yelled.

The boy turned around without stopping, flashing them an apologetic smile. It was Darren Smith. "Sorry! Homeroom! Williams!" he yelled as he kept running.

"That explains everything. You okay?" Mack asked, turning to Fiona.

"Yeah, Darren gave me a shock when he rushed by," Fiona said, then, seeing Mack's expression, "What?"

Mack stifled a laugh. "Your hair" was all he could get out before cracking up. Pieces of Fiona's wavy hair were standing straight up from end to end. "The shock must've been pretty . . . hair-raising," he added with a grin.

Fiona elbowed him in the ribs before smoothing her hair back in place. At the far end of the hall, he heard a scoff from Daisy Park, Katie Adair, and Lizbeth Harris. They were the coolest, most popular girls in Willow Cove Middle School—and they were also some of the meanest.

"Looks like the Pony Patrol is ready to prance into seventh grade," Fiona said suddenly, in a voice so low that Mack wasn't even sure he had heard her correctly.

"Did you just—" he began, but Fiona put her finger to her lips. Mack saw her eyes sparkle with mischief. *Who would've thought Fiona had a snarky side?* Mack wondered. Everybody called Lizbeth and her friends the Pony Patrol because they always wore their hair in perfect ponytails—but nobody Mack knew would ever dare to say those words aloud and especially so close to them. Somehow, though, Fiona seemed completely unconcerned, even as Mack glanced furtively at Lizbeth and the other girls. Gabriella Rivera was also part of their clique. In fact, she should have been right next to Lizbeth, but Mack didn't see her anywhere. *Weird,* he thought. *Maybe she's got Mrs. Williams for homeroom too, unless she's sick or something.*

Why else would anyone miss the first day of school?

Chapter 2
A SPECIAL EXEMPTION

Gabriella clutched the edge of the sink and leaned forward, resting her forehead against the cold mirror. She closed her eyes, as if she were sleeping. Actually, Gabriella wished she were still asleep. Then she could wake up from what was surely a nightmare—or at least the weirdest dream of all time.

One. Two. Three, Gabriella counted silently. She took a deep breath and looked in the mirror. The eyes staring back at her were bright, blazing gold, without a sliver of white; they were the color of the sun on the hottest day of summer. Their tiny, round pupils, which reminded Gabriella of a cat's, were dark and unfathomable. Gabriella's stomach lurched as she shut those eyes, those strange and unfamiliar eyes. She couldn't bear to look at them; though they were beautiful and mysterious, they were definitely not human. Was she hallucinating?

"Gabriella!" her mother called again. "Move it! You're going to be late!"

Gabriella shook her head, trying to focus. Being late for the first day of school was the least of her worries.

Change, Gabriella commanded her eyes. *Change back. Change. Now.*

She took ten slow, measured breaths. Then steeling herself for whatever truth the mirror might reveal, she opened her eyes again.

Gabriella could've cried with relief.

Her eyes were back—her ordinary, average, boring brown eyes. The same eyes that Ma called "her chocolate kisses." The same eyes that Gabriella's little sister, Maritza, had. Gabriella wasn't exactly obsessed with her looks, but she'd never been happier to stare at herself in the mirror.

There was a knock at the door.

"*Mija?*" Ma said. "You okay in there?"

Gabriella grimaced. Now, Ma didn't just sound annoyed—she sounded worried.

"Yeah!" Gabriella called. "Be right out!"

Gabriella turned the faucet on full blast and splashed cold water onto her face. Then she raked her hair into a tight, smooth ponytail. The whole time, she never looked away from her reflection in the mirror—and to Gabriella's relief, her eyes stayed the same.

This ponytail is no good, Gabriella thought suddenly. If her eyes changed at school—Gabriella didn't even want to *think* about it, but she forced herself to do so all the same—it would be totally obvious with her hair pulled back.

There was only one thing to do.

Gabriella yanked her hair out of its ponytail and fanned it around her shoulders. If she absolutely had to, Gabriella knew she could bow her head and let her hair fall in front of her face if her eyes changed at school— and she had to hide them—

The doorknob rattled. "Gabriella?" her mother asked.

Gabriella shut off the water and took one last look

at her eyes. Normal. Safe. She took a deep breath and opened the bathroom door. Ma and Maritza were standing in the hallway, waiting for her.

"Sorry!" Gabriella said, forcing her voice to sound bright and cheerful. "I was feeling a little, uh, sick, but I'm better now."

Ma nodded sympathetically. "Your stomach, huh? Nerves. I always used to get them on the first day of school. You look kind of pale, though. . . ." She reached out and pressed her hand against Gabriella's forehead. Normally, Gabriella would have ducked away, but she stood very still and let her mother check to see if she had a fever, like she used to when Gabriella was little, before Maritza was born. Back then, Gabriella used to think her mom could fix anything. Now, though, Gabriella knew better. She remembered those glowing cat eyes staring back at her from the mirror and looked down.

"Nice and cool," Ma said, and Gabriella could tell she was trying to decide if Gabriella needed to stay home.

"I'm good for school, Ma," Gabriella said quickly. What would be the point of hiding out in the house all day? Just in case her eyes got weird again? Besides,

Coach Connors would be beyond mad if Gabriella wasn't at soccer practice.

"You sure?" asked Ma.

"Positive," Gabriella said.

"Okay," Ma said finally. "Let's go. I'll drop you off."

Gabriella slung her backpack over her shoulder and followed her mother to the front door. She paused for a moment before stepping into the sunshine. Maybe it *would* be safer to stay at home . . . just in case her eyes changed again.

But Gabriella knew she would have to face school—and her friends—eventually.

When it was time for lunch, Gabriella breathed a sigh of relief for the first time all day. She was in the home stretch now: five classes done and her eyes hadn't changed, not even once. Gabriella knew that for a fact because she'd taken a peek in her compact mirror whenever she thought she could get away with it. She'd even dashed to the bathroom twice between classes—just to be sure. After Gabriella grabbed her lunch tray and headed over to her usual table, she was ready to forget all about her eyes. That was good because Gabriella could see that she had a new problem to deal with: a backpack blocking Gabriella's regular seat next to Lizbeth.

That was a bad sign.

"Hey," Gabriella said, hoping Lizbeth would move the backpack as soon as she noticed her. Hoping it had just been a mistake.

Lizbeth looked up. Her eyes grew wide at the sight of Gabriella. *Is it my eyes?* Gabriella wondered anxiously. If they had changed, Lizbeth would notice. She noticed *everything.*

"Did you . . . want to sit here?" asked Lizbeth.

"Yeah," Gabriella said, but it came out sounding like a question. "Is that okay?"

Lizbeth pursed her lips. "It's just . . . I haven't even *seen* you," she said. "You didn't come to my locker before school, you are *obviously* ignoring the text I sent last night about your hair—"

Ponytails. Of course. Everyone else at the table had one. Gabriella set down her tray and awkwardly pulled her hair back into her fist. "My elastic broke," she said quickly. It was surprising how easily the lie came to her.

"Ohhhh," Lizbeth said. She flashed her most dazzling smile as she pulled an extra elastic off her wrist. "Why didn't you say so?"

As soon as Gabriella pulled her hair into a ponytail, Lizbeth moved the backpack. Gabriella slipped into the now-empty chair and started eating. With her mouth full, Gabriella knew she wouldn't have to join Lizbeth in mocking everyone else in the caf.

Near the end of lunch, Lizbeth held out her hand. "Give me your schedule," she ordered Gabriella.

Gabriella dug it out of her backpack and obediently handed it over.

Lizbeth scanned the crumpled paper and then wrinkled her nose. "'Independent Study: Physical Education'?" she asked. "What's that? Like, 'Jock Gym for Superjocks'?"

Jock Gym for Superjocks actually sounded like a class that Gabriella would love to take, but she couldn't let Lizbeth know—especially when there was a jealous glint in Lizbeth's baby-blue eyes. Instead, Gabriella sighed heavily, as if she were dreading her next class. "It's in the ancillary gym," she pointed out. "Can you imagine? What a dump."

It was the right thing to say. Lizbeth's expression immediately changed from envy to sympathy. "You poor thing. I can't believe they haven't torn down the ancillary gym yet."

"Yeah!" Daisy spoke up. "It should be condemned!"

Lizbeth fixed an icy stare on her. "Why are you talking?" she asked.

When Daisy clamped her mouth shut, Gabriella knew that she wouldn't say a word for the rest of the day. A hot rush of anger flared inside her. *Who does Lizbeth think she is?* Gabriella thought. She was about to say something when she suddenly remembered exactly who Lizbeth Harris was: the mayor's daughter. The most popular—and most powerful—girl at Willow Cove Middle School. And the meanest, too. One wrong word from Gabriella, and Lizbeth would destroy her.

It was safer to keep her mouth shut.

Just then, the bell rang. Lunch was over. Gabriella had never been so grateful to escape from the cafeteria—not even on fish sandwich day.

Thanks to Lizbeth, Gabriella didn't need to check her

schedule to know that her next class was in the ancillary gym. Though she played three sports at Willow Cove Middle School—soccer, basketball, and softball—and ran track, Gabriella had never been inside the ancillary gym before. She had often wondered what was inside that dark and deserted building and behind those padlocked doors.

Today, though, the locks were gone, and the building blazed with lights. A woman stood in front of the doors with her hands behind her back. She wore a purple tunic over simple dark pants; her black-and-silver hair had been twisted into a thick braid that cascaded down her back. The woman's eyes seemed to see right through Gabriella, as though they were looking into her soul.

"Gabriella Rivera," the woman said with a slight nod. "Welcome."

"Hi," Gabriella replied, wondering how the woman knew her name. "Is this—"

"Go inside," she interrupted. "The others are already here."

Gabriella pulled open the doors and stepped inside

the ancillary gym. With that first step, all her expectations vanished. The ancillary gym wasn't a run-down, dilapidated, old dump. It was clean and bright inside, with gleaming equipment that looked new: balance beams; hurdles; punching bags; scratchy, yellow climbing ropes; and shiny rings that dangled from the ceiling. At the far side of the room, a large pool rippled with clear, blue water.

This is insane, Gabriella thought as a grin spread across her face. The gym was perfectly equipped for high-intensity training. How was it possible that the ancillary gym stayed locked up all the time? Nobody else at Willow Cove Middle School even knew about the pool—Gabriella was sure about that. The swim team always had to take a bus to practice in the high school pool. There had to be some reason why the ancillary gym was such a well-kept secret, but in that moment, Gabriella didn't even care. *If this is Jock Gym for Superjocks, sign me up!* she thought.

"Go take a seat with your friends," the woman said as she joined Gabriella inside the gym. Gabriella turned around fast, half expecting to see Lizbeth, Daisy, and

Katie behind her. Her tense shoulders relaxed when she realized that the teacher meant the other students in the class: Makoto Kimura, Darren Smith, and Fiona Murphy. Gabriella knew them—barely. She wouldn't exactly call them her friends.

"Sure," Gabriella replied quickly, and then crossed the gym to the single metal bench where the others were sitting in a row. Darren moved over a little, smiling at Gabriella as he made room for her. That's when Gabriella realized that the ancillary gym didn't have bleachers. Her forehead wrinkled in confusion. She'd been in a lot of school gyms—all over the state, in fact—but she'd never seen one without bleachers.

The teacher strode across the room until she was standing directly in front of the bench. Under her sharp, watchful gaze, everyone sat up a little straighter.

"I'm Ms. Therian," she said. Her voice wasn't loud, exactly, but it carried across the gym, echoing off the concrete walls, as if she had a megaphone in her hand. "This is Independent Study: Physical Education—at least, that's what the outside world thinks it is. But you all know better, don't you?"

Do we? Gabriella wondered, shifting uncomfortably on the hard bench. She had a strange feeling that this was no ordinary gym class . . . not even Jock Gym for Superjocks.

Fiona's pale hand fluttered into the air. "Gym is a requirement for graduation," she said. "Are we getting a special exemption?"

"In a manner. To everyone else at this school, you're in gym class," Ms. Therian explained. "But what you're going to be learning in this room is far more important."

A heavy silence settled over the students as they waited for her to continue.

"There's no easy way to tell you this," Ms. Therian said. "In the many years that I've taught, I've found it's best to go ahead and say it: you are Changers. What humans might call shape-shifters. And you're here to begin your training."

Gabriella blinked. *Surely* she hadn't heard correctly. . . .
Surely this was some kind of a joke. . . .
She didn't even know what a shape-shifter *was*. . . .

Mack's hand shot up. "Ms. Therian, you're kidding, right?" he asked. "I mean, shape-shifters are awesome and all, but they're about as real as . . . I don't know, superheroes or zombies . . ."

"Comic-book stuff," Darren scoffed.

Fiona stood up. "May I go to the main office?" she asked. "I need to make sure my transcript will be okay, and this definitely doesn't sound like gym class, which is a requirement for graduation, like I said, and—"

What happened next was so sudden, and so surprising, that none of the students could quite describe it. The lights of the ancillary gym flickered unevenly, as though a sudden surge of power had drawn electricity away from them. The air crackled. A brisk breeze ruffled Gabriella's hair, like a storm was brewing. But that didn't make sense; they were indoors.

There was a flash of light so blinding that Gabriella had no choice but to shield her eyes. A *fire*, she thought wildly as she caught the acrid scent of burning wires. Gabriella pulled her hand away from her face, searching desperately for the exit as her eyes adjusted.

But there was no escape, even though the doors were still unlocked. Because there, in front of the exit, stood the most massive, terrifying creature Gabriella had ever seen.

Chapter 3
The Changing Stone

The beast's sharp claws went *click, click, click* on the cold wooden floor. Gray, shaggy fur covered her tense muscles. When she turned to look at the students, she peered at them through hard, glittering eyes over a long snout.

Darren had seen wolves before—his uncle had taken him camping last winter, and for Darren, once had been enough—but this wolf was so much more terrifying than anything he could have imagined. Instinctively, he thrust his arm in front of the other kids to protect them. Gabriella batted his arm away. Darren glanced at her in confusion and got his second surprise: there was something wrong with her eyes . . . Their color and shape—

Another flash blinded Darren. Bright sparkles crowded his field of vision; he rubbed his fingers against his eyes, trying to clear his sight. As the sparkles began to fade, Darren realized the wolf was gone. In its place was Ms. Therian. She regarded them with a calm, even stare.

"Now that I have your full attention," she said, "I'll proceed. Sit down, Fiona."

Darren glanced over at Fiona out of the corner of his eye. She was so shocked that she didn't sit until Mack tugged her arm.

"That was my Changer form," Ms. Therian explained. "You all look so alarmed. I assure you that you're not in any danger. . . . Not from me, at least. I know what I have to tell you is difficult to comprehend. But as they say, seeing is believing.

"Like I was saying, you are all Changers," Ms. Therian continued. "What does that mean? Well, it's a lot more than what they tell you in comic books."

Darren flushed as Ms. Therian looked at him.

"Each one of you can change into a unique animal, animals that humans today believe only exist in myths and folktales. With your other form comes incredible powers—powers that ordinary humans can only dream of."

Powers? Darren thought. Now he *knew* that Ms. Therian was full of crazy talk. The only power he had was the ability to sleep in past lunch.

"You are not the first of your kind, not by far. You are the next generation. In ancient times we lived openly among ordinary humans, who were grateful to us for our protection and aid. But as most things go, the humans eventually turned on us, frightened of our power. Many Changers died, but some went into hiding and survive today, through you."

Ms. Therian stopped speaking and gazed upon the students. Darren stared back, but it was impossible to even think that what she was saying could be true.

"But we can talk more about history later. For now, all you need to know is that your identity as a Changer must be kept secret at all times—not just for your own safety, but for the safety of all of us—"

"Wait."

No one was more shocked by the sound of Darren's voice than Darren himself. But he had so many questions. To be honest, he couldn't believe the others weren't speaking up. No matter what the class, Fiona always had something to say, and Gabriella wasn't exactly shy. Even Mack was kind of a chatterbox. You'd never know any of that, though, from the way they were all sitting in silence.

Darren expected Ms. Therian to scold him after he'd spoken out so rudely. But to his surprise she simply nodded and said, "Go ahead."

"How do you *know* we're . . . What? Changers?" he said. "I mean, we have *nothing* in common. Why us? How can you be so sure?"

"We've known since the day you were born," she said. "It runs in families. Sometimes it skips a generation, or even several generations. Sometimes a girl will have the ability, but her sister will not. The point is, there are so few Changer families left that it's not hard for us to track them. Of course, every so often there's an aberration and a spontaneous new line of Changers emerges. They are a bit more challenging to track, but we do our best."

Fiona raised her hand. Ms. Therian nodded at her.

"My brain says this isn't possible," Fiona began. "It defies every law of science ever written. But I saw . . . I *saw* . . ."

Fiona's voice began to falter, but Ms. Therian waited patiently for her to continue.

"I can't do that," Fiona said finally, gesturing to Ms. Therian. "Whatever this ability is, I don't have it."

"You do," Ms. Therian replied. "It may not have shown itself yet, but I assure you that it's there. We find that most Changers experience their first full transformation at some point between their twelfth and thirteenth years. Of course, there will probably be signs you'll notice before a full transformation occurs, such as—"

Darren suddenly whirled around to face Gabriella. "Your eyes!" he exclaimed. "I saw them—"

Darren stopped abruptly when he realized Gabriella's eyes were an ordinary shade of brown.

"You didn't see anything," she snapped as she bent over her backpack. A small mirror glinted in her palm. "My eyes are normal."

"Gabriella, it's nothing to be ashamed of," Ms. Therian said firmly. "It's a *gift*. It won't always feel like this—changing bit by bit, out of control. You *will* learn how to master it in this class. I promise you."

Gabriella didn't say anything, but Darren saw her

return the mirror to her backpack.

Fiona raised her hand again. "So . . . what kind of Changer are you?" she asked.

For the first time since the start of class, a smile flickered across Ms. Therian's face. "You couldn't tell?" she asked. "I'm sure Makoto knows."

"Werewolf, right?" Mack guessed. "Also, could you call me Mack?"

Ms. Therian nodded. "Your grandfather used to say those comics of yours were a waste of time, but I told him he was dead wrong," she said.

"Are we all werewolves?" Darren asked, forgetting to raise his hand again. It seemed like a reasonable question, but Ms. Therian smiled.

"Of course not," she said. Then Ms. Therian reached for a leather satchel on the floor. "Would you like to find out which kind of Changer you are?"

Despite their doubts, an excited clamor arose from the kids.

With extreme care Ms. Therian reached into the satchel and pulled out an exquisitely carved box made of silver maple.

As Ms. Therian gracefully lowered herself to the floor, the students gathered around her in a circle. There was total silence as she carefully lifted the box's lid and placed it off to the side. Darren craned his neck to get a better look at what was in the box. Nestled within folds of midnight-blue silk was a large, round stone, the size of a dinner plate. It was an opaque, milky white, but as Darren gazed at it, he thought he could see brief swirls of muted colors—gray and silver and dusky lavender. He realized in that moment that this was no ordinary stone; it almost seemed to pulse with life beneath its hard, cold surface.

"It's a moonstone," Ms. Therian explained, answering the unasked question on everyone's mind, "a *true* moonstone, forged by Changer magic beneath the light of the full Eternity Moon, which comes once every thousand years. There are only two of these Changing Stones in the whole world. Here— Hold it and gaze into its depths, and your true form will be revealed."

No one moved. Darren glanced at the others. He could only imagine that his face was a mirror of theirs—a mix of trepidation, eagerness, and intrigue.

He was about to volunteer when Mack stepped forward.

"Me first!" he announced. There was a bit of a swagger in his walk as he approached the Changing Stone.

"Be careful," Ms. Therian warned. "Whatever the Changing Stone reveals, don't be afraid."

"No chance," Mack scoffed, but Darren had to wonder if Mack really felt so brave.

Mack sat down, holding the Changing Stone in his upturned palms. After several long seconds the Changing Stone began to emit a shimmering light that pulsed and quivered as the shape of a fox appeared above Mack. It was a fearsome beast, with unnaturally bright eyes and a long, plush tail. The fox's red fur bristled as it growled. But the most remarkable thing about the fox was its paws: They blazed with fire.

"*Kitsune*," Ms. Therian announced. "The *kitsune* comes from Japan, where it was renowned for the ability to fly, create illusions, and control fire . . . among other things."

Mack whispered something—something that sounded like "my dream"—but Darren couldn't be sure that he'd heard him correctly.

"Gabriella next," Ms. Therian said.

This time the image appeared the moment Gabriella's long fingers grasped the Changing Stone: a sleek and powerful jaguar with fur as dark as a moonless night. It prowled on velvety paws, staring at the kids with glittering gold eyes. The eyes, at least, were familiar to Darren; he'd seen them in Gabriella's face just moments ago.

"*Nahual*," Ms. Therian announced. "Hailing from Central America, mainly Mexico, many *nahual* take the form of the dog. A jaguar form is more rare. The black jaguar rarest of all."

Ms. Therian paused, as if to let that information sink in. "*Nahuals* are renowned for their strength, speed, and powerful healing skills," she explained. "That, and the ability to spirit walk into the dreams and thoughts of others."

At last Gabriella looked up from the Changing Stone. Darren noticed right away that her eyes were flashing gold light—and he wasn't the only one.

"Your eyes!" Mack exclaimed.

A quick look of panic crossed Gabriella's face as she thrust the Changing Stone at Fiona.

"It's all right, Gabriella," Ms. Therian reminded her. But Gabriella's eyes had already turned back to brown.

Fiona took a deep breath as she grasped the sides of the Changing Stone and peered into it. This time, the light that shone from the Changing Stone was different: watery, almost, like the reflection of the sun on the ocean.

There was the sound of a sudden splash, and for a moment Darren thought he could feel salt spray on his face; it was that real. The animal that appeared before them was clever and quick, darting in and out of the water with such speed that it was just a streak of gray. It paused at one point, staring directly at Darren with dark, glittering eyes filled with wisdom.

"The *selkie*; a seal," Ms. Therian said. "From the coasts of Ireland and Scotland, the *selkie* has a unique magical connection; it can sense when other Changers or magical beings are nearby. Their powers are concealed within their songs, which they can use to control tides, summon weather, and even bind the magic of others."

Fiona's eyes were strangely shiny when she passed the Changing Stone to Darren. It was heavier than he'd expected. Darren felt so awkward, sitting there with a polished rock in his hands. "Uh . . . what now?" he asked.

"Just look," Ms. Therian said. "The Changing Stone will do the work."

Darren bent his head over the Changing Stone and gazed into its milky depths. At first nothing happened. As the seconds ticked away, Darren could feel the back of his neck prickle with apprehension, like he'd forgotten to study for a quiz or had blown off his chores. *They made a mistake,* Darren worried. *I'm not a Changer after all.*

He was about to push the Changing Stone away when, all of a sudden, his hands felt fused to it: Darren couldn't let go. He tried to swallow, but his mouth was too dry.

Darren stared into the shimmering light and watched as a shape began to take form. The light shook, stretched wide, and then contracted into a tight ball. Just when Darren didn't think he could stand another moment of suspense, a bird burst from the Changing Stone. It was no ordinary bird, though: its eyes pulsed with otherworldly power from beneath a crest of sharp feathers that led down to a pointed beak. White feathers sat sleekly against the bird's body, darkening into shades of gray and black along its massive wings. But Darren scarcely noticed them. All he could register was the bird's claws: razor-sharp talons, glinting like platinum.

The bird flapped its massive wings as it spiraled toward the ceiling. Then it threw back its head and shrieked so loudly that everyone covered their ears—except for Darren, whose hands were still stuck to the Changing Stone. Then it happened: crackling bolts of white-hot lightning burst from the bird's claws and ripped through the air. They were about to make contact with the Changing Stone—and Darren. Even in that moment—that overwhelming, terrifying moment—Darren knew what would happen to him if lightning hit the Changing Stone while it was still in his hands: instant electrocution.

No, he thought, and just like that his fingers went limp, and the Changing Stone slipped from his grasp.

Everything happened at once.

Fiona gasped, turning her head away.

Ms. Therian cried out, a harsh word in a strange language, and dove across the floor to catch the Changing Stone before it crashed to the floor.

And the bird vanished as suddenly as it had appeared.

Total silence filled the gym, pressing down on Darren and everyone else. An uncomfortable warmth crept up his neck as everyone stared at him—everyone except Ms. Therian, who was frantically examining the Changing Stone. I *didn't mean to drop it*, he thought defensively. It *just happened*.

"No harm," Ms. Therian said at last. "Thankfully."

"Sorry," Darren mumbled all the same.

Ms. Therian continued as if she hadn't heard him. "The *impundulu*," she announced. "Or lightning bird, from the tribes of South Africa. Among the *impundulu's* many powers, perhaps the most important is the ability to impact the weather," Ms. Therian said. "The *impundulu* can generate thunder from a clap of its wings and—as we all saw—shoot lightning from its claws."

Darren held up his hands, staring at them in wonder. His fingernails were ragged from where he chewed them, a bad habit he just couldn't shake. It was hard to believe he'd be able to shoot *lightning bolts* from them.

"And so the first secrets have been revealed to us," continued Ms. Therian. "A *kitsune*, a *nahual*, a *selkie*, and an *impundulu*. Starting tomorrow, we will begin your training. In time—yes, Mack?"

Darren glanced over to see Mack waving his hand urgently. "Can we transform today?" he asked.

"I'm afraid not," Ms. Therian replied. "Transformation is different for each of us. There's no rule book; no set of instructions to follow."

The hint of a frown flickered across Mack's face. "But couldn't you just *tell* us how to do it?" he pressed.

"No one can *tell* you how to transform," Ms. Therian said patiently. "Could I tell you how to make your heart beat? Or how to make your bones grow? Such a thing would be impossible—and yet your heart beats every second, and your bones grow according to their own secret timetable, unknown to you. It is the same with Changing: when you are ready, it will happen."

Mack didn't look happy with the answer, and Darren had to admit he felt the same way. Before anyone else could ask a question, Ms. Therian turned to Fiona.

"It's different for you," she continued. "*Selkies* cannot change on their own. They need—"

"A cloak," Fiona said in a quiet voice. "I know."

An unexpected light flashed through Ms. Therian's eyes. "You do?" she asked.

"My mother," Fiona said. "When I was little she used to tell me stories about the *selkies* that swam off the coast of Ireland. I still remember the lullaby she used to sing to me at bedtime: 'Lo, *the poor selkie, alone and adrift, seeking her cloak by the base of the cliff...*'"

Fiona's voice trailed off unexpectedly, and a pink flush crept into her cheeks. She had a beautiful singing voice; Darren didn't know why she looked so embarrassed.

"What else did she tell you?" Ms. Therian asked.

"Nothing, really," Fiona replied, staring at the floor. "She died when I was three."

There was a long pause before anyone spoke again.

"A *selkie* is born with a special sealskin cloak," Ms. Therian finally said. "Without it he or she will stay in his or her human form forever. I take it, Fiona, that you don't have your cloak?"

Fiona shook her head. "I don't think so," she admitted.

"You'd know," Ms. Therian said. "So, for you, Fiona, the first step toward transformation will be finding your cloak. Without it, all this"—Ms. Therian held her arms wide—"will be of no use to you."

There was something in Ms. Therian's voice—a dangerous edge, hard as flint—that made Darren, and the others, pay close attention.

"But," Fiona began, looking puzzled. "Where could it be? Why—why don't I have it?"

Ms. Therian sighed. "It's very common for *selkies* to have their cloaks stolen and then hidden by well-meaning humans," she said, choosing her words carefully. "I can guarantee that whoever did it loves you very much. But that doesn't matter, does it, if you are forever trapped in your human form and never able to transform into your other self?"

Chapter 4
THE FORGOTTEN LULLABY

The bell rang then, but no one moved. "It goes without saying that everything we've spoken of today is to be kept in the greatest confidence," Ms. Therian reminded them. "I will see you tomorrow." And with that she turned and then exited the gym, leaving the kids alone.

"Could this really be real?" Fiona asked, breaking the silence.

"I know what I saw," Darren said. "She became a wolf. And even if that was some kind of trick, Gabriella, your eyes . . ."

Gabriella sighed. "I guess my eyes kinda make sense now."

While everyone stood stunned, Mack's face broke into a huge grin. "Guys, we have superpowers! Doesn't any of this sound the least bit cool to you?"

"Maybe," Gabriella said hesitantly. "Who knows? Maybe this might help my soccer game. Imagine what it would be like running faster, jumping higher, roaring as a jaguar . . . It seems kind of fun."

"I just can't get my head around it," Fiona jumped in. "How could the Changers have kept their powers under wraps for so long? And what happened to make the Changers go into hiding in the first place? I mean, Ms. Therian explained the general reason, but there had to have been some kind of incident, or someone who turned the humans against the Changers. . . ."

"Looks like Ms. Therian left us with more questions than answers," Darren said, standing. "Guess we'll have to wait until tomorrow to ask them, though."

The kids exchanged cell numbers and promised to text if anything out of the ordinary happened. Then they went their separate ways.

After she got her books out of her locker, Fiona went to her usual seat on the bus: right behind the driver, in the front row. She'd been sitting in that same seat, alone, since the very first day of kindergarten. Back then, Fiona used to be disappointed when no one wanted to sit next to her. Now, though, she didn't mind. Having the whole seat to herself meant that she had plenty of room to spread out her books and get a head start on her homework. Fiona's house, a shingled cottage just a block from the beach, was the very last stop on the bus route.

Fiona was the first one home, but that was no surprise; her dad had started school today too, teaching English at New Brighton University, which was an hour away. But it would've been nice if someone had been there to ask her about the first day of school.

Since she'd already finished her homework on the bus, Fiona hung her backpack on the hook next to the front door. Then she looked in the pantry. There wasn't a ton of food there—her dad had been too busy prepping for his classes to go to the grocery store over the weekend—but Fiona spotted a box of spaghetti and a jar of tomato sauce. *Perfect*, she thought. *Dinner is served.* Her father didn't exactly love spaghetti for dinner, but it was one of the quickest meals that Fiona knew how to make, and he always told her that she should never let dinner prep get in the way of her schoolwork. And *finding my selkie cloak is my schoolwork,* Fiona reminded herself.

Now, Fiona thought. *Where should I look?*

It would've helped if Fiona had any idea what, exactly, a *selkie* cloak looked like. The good news was that the cottage where Fiona and her dad lived was small. Snug, even. She might finish searching before her dad got home.

Fiona knew there was no chance the *selkie* cloak was in her own bedroom: she kept it impeccably tidy, with everything stored in precisely the right place. The living room was easy to search, too—a couch, two comfortable old chairs, a wall of bookshelves, and a television. Fiona peeked under the worn, woolen rug that covered the bare wood floor. Then she knocked on each floorboard, just in case one was loose. If *she* was going to hide something, tucked under the floorboards seemed like a safe place. But every board was securely nailed down.

Fiona wandered back into the kitchen, but she didn't have much hope of finding the *selkie* cloak there. She couldn't imagine hiding something as important and special as a *selkie* cloak over the oven or behind the fridge. Fiona thumped on the walls, just in case, searching for a hidden nook—and finding nothing.

That left the attic and her father's room. Fiona tapped her lip, lost in thought. The attic . . . Now, that had potential. The dusty attic was full of castoffs—old school projects and broken furniture and Grandpa Murphy's record collection. But to access the attic, Fiona would need to get the ladder, and she probably couldn't search all of it before her dad got home, which would lead to questions about why she was even *in* the attic . . . questions she would rather not answer right now.

So her father's bedroom was the next best choice.

As she passed the large bay window that overlooked the ocean, Fiona glanced at the driveway. There was still no sign of her dad's car, so she continued on toward his bedroom. He'd never said she wasn't allowed to go into his room, but Fiona knew she was snooping around. And that, she knew, was something her dad *definitely* wouldn't like.

She started with the dresser. Work clothes, church

clothes, weekend clothes—all neatly folded. The bottom drawer, though . . . That one was stuck. Fiona yanked and yanked, but it wouldn't budge. Is *it locked?* she wondered. But there was no keyhole.

Fiona gave one more tug on the drawer, and without warning, it shot open, sending her flying across the floor. But Fiona wasn't all that went flying. Dozens of yellowed photographs soared through the air, swirling around Fiona like snow. There were so *many* of them; photos she'd never seen before in her *life*.

Of course, she recognized her parents immediately. Her dad looked the same, except his hair was darker back then. And her mother . . . Well, Fiona would know that face anywhere. She looked exactly the same in the photos as she did in Fiona's memories of her, unchanged over the last nine years. *That's how death works,* I *guess,* Fiona thought. *It stops time.*

Time stopped for Fiona as she crouched, staring at each photo—studying them, really, as if she could memorize the photos as easily as math equations or spelling words. There was one of her parents on their wedding day, not a hundred yards from the cottage, overlooking a sparkling sunset on the ocean. Her mom cradling baby Fiona. Her dad helping Fiona ride her tricycle for the first time. And Fiona's favorite of all: her mom holding her as they sat on Broad Rock, a large, flat rock in the little beach cave near the ocean. She could remember sitting there with her mother. Fiona still went to Broad Rock whenever she missed her and wanted to feel closer to her.

How have I never seen these photos before? Fiona wondered. It would've been so nice to have pictures of her mother in the living room or in her own bedroom. To see her face in the present, not just in the past. But for some reason, her father had hidden them away, where no one could see them. Not no one, actually, because he knew where they were. He could look at them whenever he wanted. No, he was keeping them from *Fiona*.

The thought bothered her for a bunch of reasons, but before she could sort through them all, Fiona realized something else: these photos weren't the only secret that had been kept from her. *If I was given a selkie cloak as a baby,* she thought, *then someone—Mom or Dad, or both—knew the truth about me. Have known it for years.*

The idea was so unsettling that Fiona rocked back on her heels. *Were they* ever *planning to tell me?* she wondered. *Did Mom know—and the knowledge died with her? Or does Dad?*

Did they hide away my selkie cloak?

Whatever the answers were to those questions, Fiona wasn't sure she wanted to know them. And she didn't have time to ponder them, not with the sound of her dad's tires crunching over the broken shells that paved their driveway. Fiona scrambled to her feet in a flurry. It was later than she thought. And if her father found her in here with these hidden photos scattered all over the place . . .

In moments Fiona had shoved them all back into the drawer—all except for one. She tucked the photo of her mom and her at Broad Rock into her back pocket. Surely her dad wouldn't notice that it was missing. And for Fiona to have one, just *one* photo of Mom . . .

Fiona was out of breath when she reached the kitchen, just as her father opened the door. He was whistling.

"Oh!" Fiona exclaimed in surprise. "Spaghetti. I forgot to start the water boiling. . . ."

"No matter, Fee," Mr. Murphy said, handing her a box of pizza. "Didn't you get my text?"

Fiona shook her head. "I, um, left my phone in my backpack."

"I thought we should celebrate tonight!" he said. "The first day of seventh grade is a pretty big deal."

Fiona grinned as her dad nodded toward the sink. "Go ahead and wash up. I'll set the table." Then he started whistling again—a melody Fiona would've known anywhere. Her mom had sung it to her every night when Fiona was little. It was burned into the deepest recesses of her brain. Somehow, after all these years, she even remembered the words—some of them, at least.

> Betwixt the cold and rocky shoal,
> And the foam upon the sea,
> There lies a prize for my wee babe,
> It will bring her home to me.

When Dad returned to the kitchen a few minutes later, all the bubbles had disappeared down the drain, but Fiona still stood at the sink, rubbing her hands absentmindedly under the faucet. Dad chuckled as he leaned over and turned off the water. "I think they're clean now," he teased her.

Fiona managed a smile. "Sorry," she said. "I got a little distracted." What she didn't say, though, was that the thoughts triggered by that long-lost lullaby might have just solved her riddle.

The next morning Fiona woke before dawn and dressed in the gray light. She crept through the house as quietly as she could, easing out the door without making a sound. The seagulls' shrill cries called to her, and soon Fiona was running down a familiar path, past the scrubby pines that were stunted by salt spray, down the sand-strewn cliff, straight to the mouth of the cave. Straight to Broad Rock.

There was a damp chill in the cave, and the air was still and heavy. During high tide the water could seep all the way through the shadowy cave, to the darkest corners that Fiona had never dared to explore.

Now, though, it was low tide; Broad Rock was dry, and so was the sand around it. Fiona placed her palm against the stone, worn smooth from centuries of tidewater lapping against it, and closed her eyes. She would give anything to sit here with her mom again. Anything.

But Fiona knew that such a thing would never happen. She opened her eyes and reached into her pocket for the large serving spoon she'd snuck from the kitchen. A trowel would've been better, but Fiona didn't want to waste time getting one from the shed.

Fiona began to dig up the sand at the base of Broad Rock, singing under her breath as she did so. The sound of her voice echoing through the cave was haunting, as though she were listening to her own mother's lullaby long ago. Dig, scoop, dig, scoop. The rhythm was hypnotic; soon, Fiona lost track of everything else: the scrape of the spoon against the sand, the glint of the rising sun off the ocean, even the rising tide that lapped at her ankles, soaking her shoes.

Suddenly—*thunk.*

The spoon hit something solid, buried deep within the sand. Not metal on rock, but the solid, dense thud of wood. A jolt of electricity coursed through Fiona. She dropped the spoon and began digging with her hands, scooping up big fistfuls of sand and throwing them to the side until she had unearthed a chest made of grayish-tan driftwood, with rusted brass hinges. *All those hours I've sat on Broad Rock,* Fiona thought in wonder, *it was here the whole time.*

A little more digging, and Fiona was finally able to lift the chest from the sand. Her breath caught in her throat as she eased the rusty clasps open. The pile of gray material wasn't much to look at, but to Fiona it was the most beautiful thing she'd ever seen: her *selkie* cloak, at long last, after all these years. She stroked the material, which was velvety soft, and immediately heard a song carried to her on the wind. It was in a language she'd never heard before—the song itself seemed old as time—and yet Fiona knew exactly what she was supposed to do. She wrapped the *selkie* cloak across her shoulders and began a slow and steady march toward the sea.

How could she do anything else?

By the time Fiona reached the water's edge, she was no longer herself—at least, not her human form. Her mind was still intact, but little by little, all that thinking began to drift away. Was she walking? Was she swimming? Fiona didn't know. The only thing she was sure of was that she had never, in all her life, ever felt so free. The icy ocean was as soothing as a warm bath. As a *selkie*, Fiona glided smoothly through the choppy waves, bobbing and dancing over the swells with easy joy. She opened her mouth to laugh and then laughed harder at the harsh, barky sound that was her new voice. Who could care about the silly human world back on shore, with its alarm clocks and school buses and backpacks full of homework? This was all that mattered: the swell of the sea, the glorious song echoing through her heart, and the powerful propulsion of her strong tail that could take Fiona anywhere that water flowed. It was better than bliss. It was perfection.

One thought—just one—ricocheted through Fiona's mind.

What if I never went back?

Chapter 5
THE SELKIE CLOAK

"Fiona!"

The voice cut through wind and water, echoing in Fiona's round seal ears. She knew that voice. It was her father, calling to her from the rocky cliff overlooking the sea.

"Fiona!"

This time she could clearly hear the panic in his voice. All thoughts of staying a seal vanished.

In her *selkie* form, Fiona could hold her breath long enough to stay underwater as she swam past her father, who was still scanning the beach for her. As soon as she was out of his sight, Fiona pulled herself onto the shore and wriggled out of her *selkie* cloak. It was harder to take off than to put on. Fiona felt a strange ache in her limbs as she peeled the cloak away. But there she was again— two arms, two legs. No flippers.

"Fiona! Fiona, where are you?"

Fiona's icy fingers fumbled as she folded the cloak into a small square and tucked it under her dripping sweater. Her drenched clothes were the perfect way to conceal the cloak as she trudged up the cliff to her father. Now that Fiona had found her cloak, she knew she would never be apart from it again—no matter what.

"Fiona!"

"Dad!" she yelled. "I'm here!"

"Fiona! You're soaked to the bone!" Mr. Murphy exclaimed as he hurried toward her. He draped his jacket across her shoulders. "Oh my girl, what happened? Why were you in the ocean?"

"I—I fell in," Fiona said. Fiona hated lying to her father, and this lie was even harder to tell because it was so dumb. She held her breath as Mr. Murphy's expression shifted from relief to disbelief.

"You fell in?" he repeated.

Here it comes, Fiona thought. She should've known

her father would never have believed that.

"Do you have *any* idea how much danger you were in?" Mr. Murphy continued. "I'm even more terrified now than when I couldn't find you! You know better than to go into the ocean alone! You shouldn't even be at the beach without an adult present. There's no lifeguard here. The tide—"

Fiona stared at the ground as her father's voice broke. Now, she felt doubly bad. Not only had she worried her father half to death, she'd lied to him, too. "I'm sorry, Dad," she whispered. But even as she said those words, the *selkie* cloak shifted under her sweater, and Fiona knew she *wasn't* sorry: not for finding the cloak, not for trying it on, and certainly not for being who—or what—she was. If only she could explain everything to him . . . but Fiona knew that wasn't possible.

"I need to know you won't ever again go into the ocean without me," Mr. Murphy said.

"But Dad—"

"No buts, Fiona. Promise me."

I *can't!* she thought miserably. Fiona turned and stared out at the ocean, where she had felt so free. So alive. Fiona couldn't give it up—not for anything. As she stared at the pink sunrise spilling over the white-capped water, Fiona thought she saw something bobbing along the waves. What *was* that? She squinted as she tried to get a better look.

Was that the sleek head of a copper-colored seal, watching her with bright black eyes?

"Promise me, Fiona," Mr. Murphy repeated, pulling Fiona's shoulder as he gently turned her to face him. "This is important."

"I promise," she said as she whipped back around to stare at the ocean again. The copper-colored seal—if that's what it was—had already disappeared.

Mr. Murphy wrapped Fiona in a hug. "Thank you," he said. "If anything happened to you . . ."

"I'll be fine, Dad," she said. In that moment Fiona had no qualms about keeping her promise. It was a simple thing, after all—to stay out of the water when she was in her human form.

When she was a *selkie*, though?

That was a different matter altogether.

Later that day, Fiona ran into the ancillary gym, cradling her backpack like a precious, fragile thing. "I found it!" she cried gleefully. "I found my *selkie* cloak!"

"So soon?" Ms. Therian asked in surprise.

Fiona nodded. "It was buried in a beach cave near my house," she explained. "I don't know why I thought to look there. I just did. I dug and dug until I hit a driftwood box and—"

"Where is it?" Mack interrupted.

Fiona patted her backpack proudly. "Right here," she said.

"You brought it to *school*?" Gabriella asked. There was something in her voice that made Fiona bristle.

"Of course," Fiona snapped. "I'll never be away from it again."

"That's very common for *selkies*," Ms. Therian spoke up before Gabriella could respond. "The thought of losing their cloaks is too painful to contemplate. You must take precautions, though, Fiona. No one must know what you carry with you."

"I'm going to sew a secret pocket into my backpack for it," Fiona explained.

"Very good," Ms. Therian said. "Well, go ahead. Show us the cloak."

Gabriella, Mack, and Darren all leaned closer as

Fiona carefully unzipped her backpack.

"It's—this—" Fiona said awkwardly, suddenly shy as she held out her *selkie* cloak. The material spilled out of her hands, as though it were made from water.

"That's it?" Mack sounded a little disappointed. "I thought it would have, like, flippers and stuff."

"It's a *selkie* cloak, not a costume—and a beautiful one," Ms. Therian told him before turning back to Fiona. "If you'd like to transform . . ."

Fiona blinked in surprise as Ms. Therian gestured toward the pool.

"Really?" Fiona asked. "I could . . . here? Right now?"

"If you wish," the teacher replied. "The pool is salt-water, custom-calibrated for you. I think it would be a good opportunity for you to transform under my super-vision. I'm sure you've been eager to try the cloak. It is your birthright, after all."

"Actually . . . ," Fiona began, "I did try it. Early this morning."

Ms. Therian's face was blank as a stone. "And?"

"It was amazing," Fiona said breathlessly, her eyes shining. "I can't begin to tell you . . ."

"Show us, then," Ms. Therian said.

Fiona dropped her backpack and stripped down to her swimsuit, which she'd worn underneath her clothes, just in case she had time for another swim in the ocean after school. Then in one swift motion, she wrapped the *selkie* cloak around her shoulders. The other students' faces were a mixture of fascination and fear as they watched her transform, but Fiona didn't notice— or maybe she just didn't care. That beautiful song—just snatches of it, not as clear and vibrant as before—called to her again. When the transformation was complete, the same feeling of lighthearted peace and absolute certainty settled over her.

As Fiona effortlessly glided through the water, she could still hear everything happening on the surface. That's how she knew that the others were standing by the side of the pool, clapping and cheering her name.

Well done, Fiona, Ms. Therian's voice echoed in her head. *Please come join us.*

Reluctantly, Fiona pulled herself out of the pool and shrugged off the *selkie* cloak. It was even harder to remove it this time, but only because Fiona hated transforming back. She stole a glance at the pool, wishing for five more minutes as a *selkie*, or even just one. One more minute in the water . . .

"Your cloak, please," Ms. Therian said, holding out her hand.

Fiona hesitated.

"I'll just hold it while you dry off," Ms. Therian assured.

At last Fiona turned over her *selkie* cloak and stood before the others, drenched and dripping. There was a stack of towels in a basket by the pool, but Fiona didn't mind being wet. She watched warily as Gabriella strode toward her, but when Gabriella held up her hand for a high five, Fiona knew that everything was okay.

"That was *amazing*," Gabriella announced. "Fiona! You were crazy out there! Like a real seal!"

Mack and Darren hurried over too, patting Fiona on the back and laughing as her long hair dripped on them.

"Incredible," Darren said. "That was intense."

"I can't *wait* to transform!" Mack exclaimed. "Awesome, Fiona. Pretty much the coolest thing I've ever seen. *Ever.*"

Ms. Therian approached Fiona with a towel. "It was

an effortless transformation," she said. "How does it feel to become a *selkie*?"

Fiona beamed. "I love it," she said. "When I'm in the water, I never want to change back."

"Yes. I could tell," Ms. Therian said. Her lips were set in a thin, tense line. "Let's all sit for a few minutes."

Fiona wrapped the towel across her shoulders as she sat next to Gabriella.

"It's not my intention to dampen your enthusiasm," Ms. Therian began, "but I need you to understand that transformations are one of the most dangerous experiences for young Changers."

Dangerous? Fiona thought in confusion. *That can't be right. I've never felt better—safer, more alive—*

"You have been Changers for your entire lives," Ms. Therian explained. "Naturally, it comes as a tremendous relief to take your other form at last. It's not at all uncommon for a young, inexperienced Changer to become carried away, to completely forget all about his or her human life."

"What happens then?" Mack asked.

Ms. Therian looked troubled. "You would become the animal completely."

Chapter 6
Weird Together

Darren, sitting beside Ms. Therian, didn't even realize he'd started gnawing on his cuticle until he tasted blood. He wiped his thumb along the hem of his shirt, hoping that nobody would notice. There was a sickly gray cast to Fiona's face, which made Darren wonder just how close she'd been to losing herself.

"What do you mean—'completely'?" Gabriella's voice, very much on edge, broke the silence. "Like— completely a jaguar? Gone?"

"You would stay transformed," Ms. Therian explained. "Your Changer form would become your only form."

The students exploded with questions.

"Would we still *think* like humans? Or would our brains be, like, animal brains?"

"Would I recognize my family?"

"Can this happen at any time? How could I stop it?"

Darren's voice came last. "Could I *hurt* someone?"

Darren's question hung in the air as everyone waited for the answer. Finally, Ms. Therian sighed and said, "Yes. It's happened before."

Everyone started talking at once, until Ms. Therian finally held up her hands for silence. "Please. That's very rare nowadays. We have an established network of people whose sole responsibility is mentoring new Changers so that it *doesn't* happen. It's not a small thing to come into your powers. There will be bumps in the road. But we will be here to see you through it."

"You said 'we,'" Mack said. "Who else is in this network?"

Ms. Therian simply smiled. "You'll find out in time."

But to Darren, that answer wasn't good enough. In fact, *none* of Ms. Therian's answers were good enough— they always seemed like half-truths, or something the kids weren't old enough to handle. Only twenty-four hours ago, Darren had been a regular kid. But now? Everything had changed, and keeping this enormous secret was tearing him up inside. Special powers only *sounded* cool. For Darren, the reality was the opposite. He remembered the Changing Stone from yesterday— the shrieking *impundulu's* razor-sharp talons, the crackling bolts of lightning that shot from its claws—and shuddered.

"Ms. Therian, I don't want this," Darren announced as everyone turned to look at him.

If Ms. Therian was surprised, she didn't show it. "Don't want what, Darren?" she asked, fixing him with a steady gaze.

"These—these—*powers*, or whatever you call it," he said. "It's not for me. There has to be a way to, I don't know, give them to somebody else? Somebody who actually wants them? Maybe I could just never transform."

"I'm afraid not," Ms. Therian replied. "Being a Changer is as much a part of you as your own beating heart. And your transformation will happen, regardless of whether or not you want it."

It wasn't the answer Darren had hoped to hear—not by a long shot. His lungs were tight and achy as he tried to take a deep breath. Suddenly, a buzzing noise filled the room as the lights flickered overhead. While everyone looked up, Darren moved to chew on his nails again. But his hand never made it to his mouth. The buzzing, he realized, was coming from his hands. White-hot sparks jumped from fingertip to fingertip; electric-blue lines zigzagged across his skin. Darren stared at them in horror.

"Is this me?" he asked, gesturing to the flickering lights with his fingers. "Am I doing this?"

"Fear is powerful," Ms. Therian said gently. "Fear—and anger—is most commonly responsible for losing control. That's true for both normal humans and Changers, but you can master them."

Darren buried his head in his hands. The sparks at his fingertips didn't hurt him, but they were a reminder of his fear. He felt trapped in the worst way, until someone sat down beside him.

"You can do this," Gabriella urged him. "Look at it this way: if we're weird, at least we're weird together, you know?"

"It's better than you think," Fiona added. Her voice was clear and earnest; stronger than Darren had ever heard it before. "Trust me, Darren. If you never try, if you never experience a transformation, you'll never know how good it really feels."

"You can't give up," Mack said. "We're just getting started!"

Darren took a deep breath, and the lightning at his fingertips fizzled and died. He nodded his head. As the other kids settled onto the bench beside him, Darren caught a strange, knowing look in Ms. Therian's eye. Had she struggled with this same fear once too?

"Let's begin today's lesson," Ms. Therian said, breaking the silence. "We will start with your homework. After two weeks' time, please be prepared to present to the class about the mythology of your type of Changer. You will also write a three-page report, to be turned in with your presentation."

Mack's face fell. "A report?" he asked. "I thought our homework would be practicing transformations."

"Oh, it will be," Ms. Therian assured him. "And as you practice transforming, you'll keep a daily journal about your progress. Your journals will be due every Friday." She took out a stack of composition notebooks and passed them around.

Darren tried not to groan. Independent Study: Physical Education was turning out to be a *ton* of work. He'd never heard of a gym class with written reports and presentations.

"It sounds like a lot, I know," Ms. Therian said, staring directly at Darren and leaving him with the uncomfortable impression that she'd been reading his mind. "But I can assure you that it's all essential to your progress. In fact, it's very common for a young Changer to learn something in the mythology that helps him or her transform."

Ms. Therian stood up. "Fiona, since you already know how to transform, you may practice underwater movements in the pool," she said. "The rest of you will practice your transformations for the remainder of class and—"

"Ms. Therian," Fiona cut in. "Before we split up . . . Just before, in the pool . . . I heard your voice in my head, but I was watching you from underwater and your mouth didn't move."

"Changers communicate telepathically," Ms. Therian answered. "Though it's something that usually doesn't come before your first transformation, you will be able to communicate this way in both your Changer and human forms."

"So . . . you can read our thoughts?" Darren asked nervously.

"Not anything so dramatic," Ms. Therian laughed. "Just as you would speak when in your human form, so you can speak telepathically. You don't go blurting out every thought that comes into your head, do you? Speak with your mind; you'll get the gist of it in time."

"What are we supposed to do now?" Mack asked as Fiona walked over to the pool and Ms. Therian went along to supervise her.

Darren shrugged. "I don't know," he replied.

"This is boring," Mack said. "I mean, shouldn't *somebody* be able to tell us *something* a little more clear about transforming?"

"Maybe if you stopped talking so much, you could figure out how to change," Gabriella told him.

Darren tried not to laugh—especially when he saw

a flash of gold light up Gabriella's eyes. *She's like me,* he thought suddenly. *She's already started changing. And she doesn't know how to control it either.*

It wasn't just relief that surged through Darren then; a bolt of electricity materialized at his fingertips.

"Whoa!" Mack shouted loud enough that Ms. Therian looked over. "How'd you *do* that?"

"I—I don't even know," Darren said helplessly. "It only happens in here."

"Maybe it's because we're all together?" suggested Gabriella.

"Maybe," Darren replied.

Mack reached over to Darren, his finger hovering less than an inch from Darren's crackling hands. "I can feel the heat," Mack marveled. "I wish *kitsunes* could shoot lightning from their paws. Dude. This is so cool."

"From what we saw in the Changing Stone, you'll be able to control fire with your paws—that's pretty cool," Darren said, wondering how odd the remark sounded.

"Do you think you could make a lightning bolt hit the wall over there?"

"Nah. Not yet, anyway," Darren said, but just thinking about doing something like that made more sparks shoot from his hands. Darren smiled weakly as he pulled his hands away. Maybe the others thought it was cool, but in his heart Darren knew the truth: his powers were completely unpredictable.

And more dangerous than anyone knew.

Chapter 7
THE OTHER KITSUNE

Dinner at Darren's house was going to be quiet that night. Neither of his parents would ever tell him when they'd had yet another fight, but he wasn't stupid. He could always tell.

"Where's Dad?" Darren asked warily as he set the table.

"Oh, you know. Watching the game with his buddies," Mom said. She smiled brightly at Darren, but he didn't smile back. What was the point of smiling when it was totally fake? Darren knew full well that his mom got upset when his father skipped family dinners, which he was doing more and more often lately. *I wish Ray was here*, Darren thought as Mrs. Smith brought two plates of food over to the table.

Darren's older brother, Ray, had just started his first year of college at New Brighton University, where their mother was a chemistry professor. NBU was only an hour away, but now that Ray lived in the dorms, Darren felt like he barely saw him. Even though Darren and Ray tried to video chat at least once or twice a week, life just wasn't the same now that Ray was gone. Darren missed him like crazy.

"How was school?" Mom asked automatically as she sat down.

Darren paused with his fork halfway to his mouth, considering all the different answers he could give:

Good. I can make lightning with my fingers.

Good. I'm in a special class for half-human, half-animal freaks.

Good. I'm learning how to transform into a giant bird.

It would've been such a relief to say any of those things—to tell someone he loved and trusted the truth about what was going on. But Ms. Therian's warning about secrecy flashed through Darren's mind. In the end, all he said was, "Good."

Darren waited to see if his mom would ask more questions, but she had started flipping through a chemistry journal. Darren would never understand why his mother got to read during meals, but he wasn't allowed to use his cell phone. Darren sneaked a few glances at her while he slipped his phone out of his pocket. She didn't even notice as he sent a text under the table.

R, you around to chat tonight?

Darren took another bite of food, still holding onto his phone under the table. When it buzzed, he jumped.

Absolutely, bro. 9?

"Darren," Mom said, holding out her hand. "No phones at the table. You can have it back after dinner."

For once, Darren didn't even complain about having to give up his phone. Just knowing that he would be able to talk to Ray in a few hours made everything seem more bearable.

At 8:54 p.m., Darren was already sitting in front of his mom's laptop, waiting for Ray to sign on.

"Little D!" Ray announced as he appeared on the screen. "Big seventh grader! What's happening, man?"

A huge grin spread across Darren's face. "Not much," he said. "I'm getting slammed with homework already."

Ray chuckled. "You don't even know the meaning of the word," he replied. "I was at the library last night until four a.m."

"Are you serious?" Darren asked.

"Like a heart attack," Ray said. "But enough about me. I want to hear everything about seventh grade."

Darren started telling Ray all about his new classes but was consciously aware that he was holding something back—a lot of things, actually. He quickly changed the subject to his football practice, but Ray held up his hand.

"Hang on right there," Ray said. "I can tell you're keeping something from me. What's wrong?"

The last thing Darren wanted was for Ray to know he was keeping something back, but at the same time, it was such a relief that somebody was paying attention. And yet, as much as Darren wanted to tell Ray the truth—to show him his hands, which were at this very moment crackling with electricity under the desk—he didn't dare. The danger was too great.

But was there a way that Darren could talk to Ray without telling him everything?

"Things are kind of . . . weird this year," Darren began, choosing his words carefully. "It's almost like I don't . . . really fit in, you know?"

"Of course I do," Ray said in such a knowing way that for an instant, hope swirled through Darren's heart. *Is Ray a Changer too?* he wondered. Ms. Therian did say that it ran in families. . . .

"I was wondering when it might come up," Ray continued. "Things started to change for me in middle school too—"

Darren was hanging on Ray's every word.

"I mean, it's really pretty obvious: there aren't a lot of African-Americans in Willow Cove. And even when everybody's being cool, it's normal to feel different sometimes."

It wasn't exactly what he was hoping to hear, but Darren had looked up to Ray his whole life. Ray always had the answers before. Maybe he had the answer to Darren's real question, too, even if he didn't know it. "So . . . how did you handle it?" he asked.

"Just do you," Ray advised him. "You've already got a ton of friends, more than I ever had. That's a good start. Work hard in school, stay out of trouble. Basically, just do your best, you know? That's all Mom and Dad want from us. And speaking of Mom and Dad . . ."

Ray didn't need to finish his sentence; Darren already knew what he was going to ask. "Pretty much the same," he said. "Dad skipped dinner again tonight."

Ray made a face. "He has to step up," he replied. "He knows that drives Mom crazy. I saw Mom yesterday and tried to talk to her, but she said she was late to class and rushed off."

"Well, neither one of them is telling me anything," Darren said. "So if you find something out . . ."

"You'll be the first person I tell. You know that," Ray said.

"Thanks, Ray," Darren said. He really did feel better. With the relief came a surge of tiredness, too; it was exhausting to hold on to so much stress all the time. Darren said good-bye to his brother and then flopped down onto the bed with his social studies book. He still had to read a chapter before bed, and his mom was as strict about lights-out as she was about cell phones at the table.

But Darren found himself nodding off after the first paragraph and falling instantly into a dream.

There should've been a full moon, but a heavy cover of clouds made the night sky darker than usual. The only visible light came from the gleaming streetlights; Darren had never seen them from above before. High, low, swooping, soaring—there was nothing he couldn't see, nothing he couldn't do. Darren got it now; he understood what Ms. Therian and Fiona had tried to tell him. With every beat of his wings, Darren understood. This was his power. This was his destiny. This was his real, true self, flying over Willow Cove and seeing the world in an entirely new way.

Darren flew as low as he dared over the dark, quiet homes of Willow Cove. *What would they think if they could see me?* he wondered.

Below him, something began to stir. Were people getting up already? It was still dark out.

Uh-oh, Darren thought. He didn't want to be seen

by anyone, but he wasn't ready to stop flying, either. It wouldn't be a problem to fly over to the forest, though. Maybe he would head in that direction. . . .

But something inside him prickled at the thought of pulling away.

Darren flew lower still to see if he could find what had caught his attention, but with his incredible vision, he didn't really need to. The movement on the street sped up, but he realized suddenly that it wasn't people moving. Shadows were unfurling throughout the streets, choking the sleepy houses, seeping under doors and through windows. What was that stuff going to do to all the people asleep in their homes? They had no idea about the threat approaching them.

Only Darren knew.

And that meant only Darren could stop it.

He flew lower. It seemed like the right thing to do, but it was the worst mistake he could have made. The shadows reared back, surrounding him, grasping at his feathers, yanking at them— It hurt—

It *really* hurt.

There was a bright, brief spiral of pain, and then

Darren found himself on his hands and knees—*hands and knees*—in a wheat field outside town. It was hard to catch his breath in his human form. *Just a dream?* Darren thought. *All that crazy stuff from school has messed up my head.*

Even as he tried to convince himself, Darren longed for his strong wings. He felt utterly alone—incomplete, even—without them. Had he really flown? There was a strange ache in his shoulder blades as he pulled himself up. He would have to find his way back to town—but it would take hours to walk the distance. He must have flown—how on earth could he have sleepwalked this far, and out his second-story bedroom window no less?

Darren jumped, realizing he wasn't alone. There, at the edge of the clearing, stood the most magnificent creature Darren had ever seen. A huge, pure-white fox with fiery paws, sitting at attention with nine long tails splayed out on the ground behind it. A *kitsune*, Darren thought suddenly as he remembered Mack's projection from the Changing Stone.

The fox stepped forward, and a deep voice echoed in Darren's head. *Hello, Darren.* It was not Mack's voice.

"Who are you?" Darren asked. "How do you know my name?"

You can call me Mr. Kimura, the fox replied. *I know you have questions. Come with me, and I will answer as many as I can.*

They walked in silence for a few moments before Darren suddenly exclaimed, "Kimura! Are you Mack's grandfather?"

The fox nodded. *Smart boy. Dorina said as much.*

"How . . . ," Darren began, but he couldn't finish the sentence. There were too many things he wanted to say all at once.

You changed in your sleep and flew here on your own, Mr. Kimura explained. *What do you remember?*

"I was really tired," Darren said. "But I don't remember falling asleep. The next thing I knew, I was flying over Willow Cove. Then . . ."

The fox's ears pricked up as Darren's voice trailed off. *Go on.*

"It was a shadow, kind of," Darren said. "It was . . . bad. I wanted to stop it from sneaking into everybody's houses, but it started to attack me instead."

When Mr. Kimura didn't respond, Darren pressed on. "That part was a dream, though. . . . Right?" he asked.

The fox glanced behind them, as if worried that they were being followed. *A dream for now. We will discuss it indoors,* he said as they approached a small cottage. There was a light on in the front window. As Darren and Mr. Kimura approached, the front door swung open.

"Jiichan?" a voice called. "Is that you?"

Mack was standing in the doorway, a worried look on his face. He blinked in surprise as Darren stepped forward.

"Darren?" Mack asked. "What are you doing here?"

"Hey, Mack," Darren replied. It was all he could think of to say.

Mr. Kimura brushed past Darren as he approached Mack. *Hurry in,* the *kitsune* said in a low voice. Darren could only obey, watching as the expression on Mack's face morphed from surprise to astonishment.

"Jiichan?" Mack asked hesitantly, backing up until he was pressed against the wall.

The door closed behind them with a loud click, though Darren was certain he hadn't touched it. The next moment a shimmering light washed over them. When it passed, the majestic fox was gone.

In his place stood an old man whose eyes seemed to contain all the worries in the world: Mr. Kimura, in human form.

Chapter 8
THE FIRST FOUR

"Jiichan?" Mack gasped. He would've thought he was still asleep, stuck in the strangest dream ever, if not for the solid wall against his back. "You . . . You're a . . ."

"Yes," Jiichan replied as he strode past his grandson.

Mack stared at Jiichan, then glanced over at Darren. "You want to tell me what's going on?" he demanded.

Darren shifted uncomfortably from one foot to the other. "Uh . . ."

"Forget it," Mack mumbled as he spun around and hurried after Jiichan. He found him in the living room, the TV remote clutched in his wrinkled hand. This time, though, Jiichan wasn't watching one of his favorite nature shows. Instead he flipped to the twenty-four-hour weather network.

"We're tracking a massive category-five hurricane approaching the coast," the weather forecaster reported breathlessly. "This is not a drill, folks. We have no indication that this storm is going to shift course or slow down. I repeat, it's not weakening at all. Now is the time to start making preparations, because once this hurricane hits, it's going to be too late."

Jiichan muted the TV. Images of leveled houses, downed trees, and rescue workers sifting through rubble flashed across the screen, lighting the living room.

"Well, now you know that I am no ordinary grandfather," Jiichan said, turning to Mack. "And that, I'm afraid, is no ordinary hurricane."

"Are you going to tell us what you mean by that, or are we supposed to guess?" Mack asked. Even he was surprised by the rudeness in his voice, but only Mack knew what his bad attitude was supposed to conceal: the deepest, most unsettling surprise he'd ever experienced. All this time, Jiichan was a Changer—a *kitsune* like he was—and he'd never told Mack. It hurt a lot more than Mack wanted to admit.

"Of course I will," Jiichan replied. "Darren? Would you care to join us?"

Mack had almost forgotten that Darren was hanging back in the doorway. The boys sat next to each other on the couch, across from Jiichan. "Dorina has kept me informed about your studies," Jiichan told them. "But I know there is a great deal you still yearn to know. It appears I have no choice but to tell you about it tonight. Circumstances demand no less."

"What's going on?" Mack asked.

Jiichan nodded toward the TV. "That's not a storm," he said again. "It's an army of Changers preparing to descend on Willow Cove."

It was a crazy thing to say—it barely made any sense—but Mack had never seen such a serious look on his grandfather's face before. It chilled him to the bone.

"But to understand what's happening today, you must understand what happened in the past," Jiichan said with a heavy sigh. "Dorina told you there was a time when humans and Changers lived in harmony. We used to protect villages, summon rain for crops—even heal the sick. But one thousand years ago, an evil warlock came into being. He knew that to achieve absolute power, he would need to harness the abilities of the Changers."

"How could he do that?" Mack asked.

"The darkest magic imaginable," Jiichan said as a heaviness settled over his shoulders. He suddenly looked older to Mack than he ever had before. "The warlock forged an iron horn, carved with ancient runes we thought had been lost to history. The evil that went into creating the horn and gathering the runes is unthinkable, but when he was finished, the warlock had made the most powerful weapon in the history of magic."

"What could the horn do?"

"It bound the Changers to him, putting them at the mercy of his will. Across the land our armies fell with a single blast. The horn forced them to turn against normal humans—destroy their food, burn their homes, take their lives. Dark days followed. The darkest days our world has ever seen. Changers were powerless against the warlock's horn. There was little happiness and less hope."

Jiichan paused to let the boys take in his words.

"It wasn't until four young Changers stood against the warlock that he fell," he continued. "Four young Changers, untested and unproven, found themselves immune to the horn's call. Today they are the First Four, the leaders of all Changer-kind."

"They're still alive?" Mack broke in. "That was a thousand years ago!"

Jiichan smiled enigmatically. "You have much still to learn about our kind."

"What happened to the warlock's horn?" Darren asked.

"The horn could not be destroyed, so it was locked away, never to be used again. And that, they thought, would be the end of it. Life would go back to normal."

"But that didn't happen, did it?" asked Mack. He'd watched enough superhero movies to have a pretty good idea of what happened next.

Jiichan shook his head. "The damage had been done. Humans no longer trusted Changers. They'd seen what our powers could do, and no promises or assurances could calm them. Instead, humans decided that Changers must be hunted down and then erased from history. We became myths, folklore, the boogeymen in their children's stories. And that's why we live as we do now—lives of secrecy, spent in the shadows."

Mack clenched his fists. "That's not *fair!*" he said hotly. "It wasn't our fault."

Jiichan smiled sadly. "Sometimes the concept of magic is just too much for ordinary humans to believe. As far as people knew, Changers had tried to destroy them. They then had to live knowing we could destroy them, if we wanted to. I can't blame them. Fear makes people act in desperate ways."

"Why are you telling us this?" Darren asked suddenly. "All this stuff happened—what, a thousand years ago? Why does it matter now?"

Jiichan regarded Mack and Darren in silence. At last, he spoke. "The horn is gone," he said. "Stolen by a new warlock who goes by the name of Auden Ironbound— stronger and even more driven than his ancestor, who began the first age of destruction.

"Even now, at this very moment, Auden Ironbound and his army approach," Jiichan continued. "*That's* why it matters."

"Here?" Mack asked incredulously. "Auden Iron-bound is coming *here*? To Willow Cove?"

"Willow Cove is the final fortress against him," Jiichan explained. "This is where the First Four live. If they can't stop Auden Ironbound, no one can. He means to defeat the Four and then take the world for himself."

Mack jumped up from the couch. Even though it was the middle of the night, he had way too much nervous energy to sit still for a moment longer. "The First Four live *here*?" he asked. "Who are they?"

"You already know, Mack," Jiichan said. "In fact, you've known them your entire life."

Mack's breath caught in his throat. "Jiichan," he whispered. "You?"

Jiichan didn't speak. He didn't need to. The answer was written on his face.

This can't be true, Mack thought wildly. How was it possible that his grandfather—*his jiichan!*—was one of the most powerful Changers to ever live? Was one of the legend-ary First Four? *Was more than a thousand years old?* It was too bizarre to believe. At least it would've been if Mack didn't have a deep sense of certainty in the pit of his stomach.

Jiichan said I knew the others, Mack thought. *So who are they?* In his mind, Mack raced through just about everybody he'd met in Willow Cove, from his teachers to his pediatrician to the grumpy lady who worked at the post office. No, no, and no.

My whole life—

The realization hit Mack with tremendous force. Of course. How had he missed it? The answer was staring him straight in the face: Jiichan's mah-jongg set, neatly polished and waiting for Thursday night, when his three best friends would come over to play. But were they ever truly playing? Did he ever hear the pieces move? All Mack remembered was the low talking coming from the other room while he turned up the volume on the TV. They hadn't been discussing mah-jongg at all.

And it wasn't a coincidence that Ms. Therian and Jiichan were such good friends. No, they were friends because they were both Changers. And if Jiichan was one of the First Four, then Mack had a pretty good sense that Ms. Therian was, too. And so were Sefu Badawi and Yara Moreno, Jiichan's other mah-jongg buddies.

"Ms. Therian is one of the First Four!" Mack was

practically shouting as he turned to Darren. "And—"

"It's time to take Darren home before his family awakens and realizes he's gone," Jiichan interrupted.

Darren glanced around the room for a clock. "My dad gets up pretty early for work," he said anxiously. "What am I going to tell him if he's already awake?"

"Don't worry. He's still asleep," Jiichan said.

"How do you kn—" Mack started to ask when he suddenly thought, *Duh, of course he knows, that's probably some special* kitsune *power or something.* Mack had so many questions for Jiichan that he didn't know which one to ask first. And he wasn't alone.

"Mr. Kimura," Darren said as they piled into the car, "if there are all these secret magical beings—Changers and warlocks and stuff—does that mean that vampires are real, too?"

"What about zombies?" added Mack. "Bigfoot?"

Jiichan chuckled. "Don't be ridiculous, boys," he said. "There are Changers, humans, and what you might call witches and warlocks. That's all."

That's all, Mack thought as he glanced out the car window. A *hidden world full of magic that I never knew existed.* The sky was still heavy with clouds; in the distance he could see one of the clouds light up from within. *Lightning,* he thought. Or was it?

"Maybe we should get out of town," Darren said suddenly, making Mack wonder if Darren had also noticed the glowing cloud. "If Auden Ironbound uses the power of Changers to make himself stronger, won't he just use us, too? Why are we sticking around?"

"This is not the time to flee," Jiichan replied. "This is the time to take a stand. We must stop Auden Ironbound before he grows more powerful. Here. Now."

"You mean Darren and I are going to fight Auden too?" Mack asked in excitement.

"You and your young friends will have your role to play, but it will be far from the action," Jiichan replied.

"Aw, come on!" Mack groaned.

"No, Mack," Jiichan said in a firm voice. "The danger is too great. The First Four—who are immune to the horn—will make a stand. We should be able to defeat Auden, just as we defeated his ancestor a thousand years ago."

No one spoke again until Jiichan pulled up in front of Darren's house. It was dark and still; the rest of

Darren's family was obviously still asleep, just as Jiichan had predicted.

"Thanks for the ride, Mr. Kimura," Darren said, stepping out of the car. "I probably should've just flown home myself and saved you the trouble."

Flown home? Mack thought. *Did Darren just—*

Jiichan held up a warning finger. "Please be careful, Darren," he said. "The danger is greater for you. Should you lose control of your transformation midflight, the consequences could be disastrous. Your human form has the same limitations as anyone else, after all."

"You transformed?" Mack asked Darren. "And *flew?*"

Darren nodded. "Crazy, isn't it?"

"How?" demanded Mack.

"It happened while I was asleep," Darren admitted. "Then I flew and ended up in a field, and your grandfather was waiting for me, like he already knew I was going to be there. So, I don't really know how I transformed."

"Oh, I think you do," Jiichan said. Then he pointed up at the second-story window, which was wide open. "Go ahead."

Darren's grin lit up his entire face.

Mack watched closely as Darren shut his eyes. His

eyelids were doing something weird, Mack noticed—
fluttering, as if Darren couldn't figure out how to open
them. His face twitched twice—three times—like
something deep inside was causing him pain.

Suddenly, a shimmering ripple moved over Darren,
from his head to his feet, leaving in its wake the strik-
ing *impundulu*. The bird cocked its head, staring at Mack
and Jiichan with a glittering eye. Mack had never seen a
bird smile before, but this one sure was.

"Whoa," Mack said, amazed.

"Well done," Jiichan said, but his simple praise was
underscored by the delight in his voice.

Then, while Mack and Jiichan watched, Darren flew
up to the window and ducked inside.

Mack was silent as he and Jiichan drove home.
Watching Darren transform had impacted him in ways
he didn't completely understand. It was so glorious and
so unexpected; like living in the most exciting superhero movie ever. And yet Mack felt strangely lonely and
incomplete. When would it be *his* turn to experience a
transformation? Mack's longing to take his *kitsune* form
was greater than ever.

"You seem troubled, Mack," Jiichan said.

That's the understatement of the year, Mack thought. But what he said was, "Fiona and Darren have already figured out how to transform, but I don't even have a clue."

"In time you will find your own path," Jiichan replied calmly.

"Time? We don't have time," Mack argued, his voice rising. "You just said that Auden Ironbound is on his way to Willow Cove, like, *now*! Please, Jiichan, can't you just *tell* me how to transform? Or—better—*show* me?"

"Perhaps you should focus more on the journey than the destination," Jiichan said.

"Seriously?" Mack groaned. "Come on, Jiichan! Can't we just skip over all the pearls of wisdom and get to what really matters?"

"No, Mack," Jiichan said firmly. "My word on this is final."

Mack sighed in frustration as he twisted in his seat, staring out the window. The sky was gray now; morning was almost upon them, but Mack hardly noticed.

As much as he hated it, he knew in his heart that Jiichan was probably right.

Chapter 9
BATTLE PLANS

By the time school rolled around later that morning, Mack's bad mood had worsened. All he wanted to do was finally figure out how to transform, but he couldn't exactly work on it in the middle of English or science class. Changers class was the only thing Mack looked forward to, the one time in the entire day when he could truly be himself. *Maybe today will be the day,* Mack thought eagerly as he approached the ancillary gym.

Inside, everyone was clustered in a tight clump by the bench. Mack could tell immediately that something big had happened, but nothing could've prepared him for the sight of a full-size jaguar standing there.

Mack stood very still, too shocked to move. Even though he *knew* it was Gabriella—*So, she figured out how to transform, too,* he thought—it wasn't easy to approach such a powerful creature.

The *nahual* turned and looked at Mack with her gold cat eyes. Her long tail, covered with black fur so glossy that it almost looked blue, swished back and forth.

Not bad, huh? Gabriella's voice echoed in his head.

"Incredible," Mack said, but his voice sounded funny—hollow and small.

"Check it out!" Darren suddenly exclaimed, and *whoosh*—the *impundulu* was back. Mack forced himself to smile through the excited shrieks and chatter from everyone else, but he was painfully aware that he was the only one who still didn't know how to transform. His eyes met Fiona's, and as they stared at each other, all Mack could think was *Please don't. Please don't change.* He wasn't sure he could bear it if everyone was in his or her Changer form—everyone except him.

Somehow, Fiona seemed to understand. Her *selkie* cloak stayed neatly folded in her lap, to Mack's relief.

Ms. Therian clapped her hands loudly. "Human

forms, please," she announced, and just like that, Gabriella and Darren were back. Mack joined the others on the bench, grateful for the chance to blend in.

"There has been a significant new development," Ms. Therian announced. Then she filled in Gabriella and Fiona about everything that had happened overnight— from the full history of the Changers to Darren's strange dream to the warlock now approaching Willow Cove.

"I can't believe you flew by yourself," Fiona whispered to Darren. "Weren't you scared?"

"No," he replied with a chuckle. "I was asleep! Apparently, I'm a sleep-flier."

"Listen carefully, please, because what I am about to say affects all of us," Ms. Therian continued after a sharp look at Fiona and Darren. "The First Four met early this morning to finalize our battle plans. When Auden Ironbound arrives, Mr. Kimura will lead him to the north side of town, where there are fewer houses. Sefu, Yara, and I will hold his army at the beach. You four will be responsible for patrolling the town. Should any of Auden Ironbound's soldiers escape the beach, you'll need to alert one of us. It's important you don't try to engage them. Luckily, when the storm hits, everyone should already be evacuated or taking cover in the storm shelters, so it's our hope that none of the townspeople will be in danger."

"When is this going to happen?" Fiona asked.

"Soon," Ms. Therian said. "That's the best I can tell you right now. Time is of the essence, so I suggest we stop talking now and get to work. Fiona, I want you to practice those deep breathing exercises we discussed. Darren, flight for you today, I think. Gabriella, let's work on sprinting for you. I think you'll find it's quite a different experience on four legs instead of two. And Mack, keep practicing your transformation. I'm sure you'll have the hang of it in no time."

The moment Mack had been dreading was upon them: in a flash, everyone else transformed, leaving him behind. His face was burning as he moved to sit alone on the floor, trying with all his might to transform—fluttering his eyelids, flexing his muscles, twitching, stretching, everything. But with each move he got the same result.

Nothing.

Mack was actually glad when the bell rang, signaling the end of the school day. Since Mack didn't need to transform back into his human form, he was the first one out the door. Comics Club was meeting today, and that was always fun. Suddenly, Mack felt like he'd barely seen or talked to Joel since riding the bus on the first day of school. *Hanging out with non-Changers is just what I need,* Mack decided—until he arrived at Comics Club and saw everyone poring over the latest issue of *Super Warriors.* Superpowers, superpowers, superpowers wherever Mack turned. For the first time in his life, Mack was sick of comic books and superheroes.

"Mack! Get in here!" Joel hollered when he spotted Mack hovering in the doorway. "You won't believe what happens in issue seventeen!"

"Actually, I can't stay," Mack replied. "I have some stuff to do at home."

Joel's face fell. "Oh. Okay," he said. "Talk to you later?"

"Sure," Mack replied.

Mack sent a quick text to Jiichan to ask for a ride home and then set off for the parking lot to wait for him. The clouds had never cleared up, and now, a light drizzle was falling. It didn't seem like much, but soon Mack's shirt was soaked.

"Mack!" a voice called.

He turned around to see Gabriella approaching. He could see her friend Daisy trying to get her attention, but Gabriella didn't seem to notice her.

"Hey," Mack replied. "What's up?"

"Practice got canceled," Gabriella said, gesturing to her cleats. "The weather."

"Do you need a ride? My grandfather should be here soon," said Mack.

Gabriella shook her head. "I live close enough to walk," she said. "But I can hang out with you while you wait."

"Thanks," Mack said. He glanced over his shoulder to see if anyone was nearby, but they were alone. *Just do it*, Mack told himself. *Swallow your pride and ask.*

"Can I ask you something?" Mack said.

"Sure," replied Gabriella.

"What's it like?" Mack asked, his words tumbling out in a rush. "Changing, I mean."

Gabriella stared off into the distance, deep in thought. "It's . . . hard to describe," she began. "I've only done it twice now. I guess . . . Have you ever been bodysurfing?"

"Like in the ocean?" said Mack. "Sure."

"It kind of feels like that," she explained. "You feel this wave approaching, and then you have a choice: if you take a deep breath and, like, prepare yourself . . . and just sort of let go . . . the wave will lift you up and carry you. It's so easy and natural. It feels right, you know?"

Mack nodded.

"But if you force it, you'll face-plant," Gabriella continued. "The wave will drag you down, and you'll be sputtering through a mouth full of sand and salt water."

Gabriella pulled her hair out of its high ponytail. "I'm not sure that makes any sense," she said with a self-conscious laugh.

"No," Mack said earnestly. "You made perfect sense. I think . . . I've been doing everything wrong, you know? I've definitely been trying to force it . . . and getting nowhere."

Gabriella looked sympathetic. "I think that first transformation is kind of out of our control," she confided. "My eyes—They'd started changing on their own.

If we hadn't started Changers class right around the same time, I don't know *what* I would've done. Can you imagine how terrifying it would have been to change without warning?"

"Yeah," Mack said. "I hadn't thought about it like that before. At this point I'm just so ready to change. I can't believe I'm the last one to figure it out."

"That doesn't matter," Gabriella told him. "You'll get it. Ms. Therian believes in you—and look, your own *grandfather* is one of the First Four—I mean, that's *incredible!*"

Mack tried to smile, but Gabriella's enthusiasm just made him feel worse. If Jiichan was one of the First Four, shouldn't Mack have an easier time transforming—and not harder?

Just then, Jiichan pulled up to the curb. Mack was happier than usual to see him. If talking to Gabriella had given him an entirely new perspective on how he should approach Changing, then what could he learn from his own grandfather, a true master?

"Thanks for the advice, Gabriella," Mack said. He hopped into the car.

"How was your day?" Jiichan asked as Mack fastened his seat belt.

"Gabriella can change now too," Mack said with a sigh. "That's everybody—everybody except me. Please, you have to help me, Jiichan. Can you at least tell me what's it like? What did it feel like when you first transformed?"

Jiichan turned up the windshield wipers to high. "You will understand soon," he replied.

Mack balled up his fists in frustration. He and Jiichan sat in silence for a few moments while Mack tried to get his anger under control.

"I'm asking you simple questions!" Mack finally exploded. "Why won't you answer them? I don't know how to do this and it's killing me!"

"Perhaps, then, you should try patience," Jiichan said.

"Oh, thanks. That's great advice," Mack said sarcastically. He knew how disrespectful he was being, but for once, he was so upset that he didn't even care. "It's not like there's some insane, power-hungry warlock on the way. You're right. I'll just sit around and wait. I'm sure that will work out fine."

Jiichan didn't respond, which made Mack even angrier.

"It would've been hard enough to go through this if Mom and Dad were here," he snapped. "But they're gone. I guess it was too much to expect my grandfather to be there for me."

But not even that could get a response from Jiichan. As they drove home without speaking, Jiichan's silence made Mack feel worse than ever.

Chapter 10
THE HORN OF POWER

A famous poet was visiting the campus of New Brighton University later that evening, which meant Fiona was spending the afternoon in her father's office in the English department. As chair for poetry, her dad was always hosting readings like this. Though she was looking forward to hearing the poet read, Fiona found herself wishing she were anywhere else. Actually, just one place else: the ocean cove, where she had first swam as a *selkie*. The saltwater pool in the ancillary gym just wasn't the same.

Fiona stood up from her father's desk and decided to get a snack from the vending machine. When she saw a familiar face reflected in the glass case, she almost gasped.

"Darren?" Fiona asked in surprise. "What are you doing here?"

"Fiona!" Darren exclaimed. "I— What are *you* doing here?"

"My dad's an English professor," she explained. "He's working late tonight, so . . ."

Darren nodded knowingly. "My mom's a chemistry professor," he said. "Usually, I hang out in the science building, but man, it stinks over there today!"

"Experiment gone wrong?" Fiona laughed.

"Definitely," Darren replied. "My brother, Ray, goes here, and he said that the English department has the best student lounge."

"Oh, it does. No doubt about that," Fiona said.

"So here I am," Darren said.

"You know, I was going to head over to the library to work on my Changers report," Fiona said. "Want to come?"

"Sure," said Darren.

"Have you ever been in the rare books room before?" Fiona asked as they walked across campus. "You won't even believe the amazing ancient texts they have—parchment pages, gold lettering . . . You even have to wear cotton gloves to touch them."

"Gloves?" Darren made a face. But when they reached the library, he didn't complain when she handed him a pair.

Soon, Fiona was so engrossed in the beautiful old books that she almost forgot Darren was there. The only sound was the camera on her phone, *click-click-click*ing as she took photos of anything she could find on *selkies*.

Then Fiona gingerly opened an ancient book with a crumbling cover. It was like an encyclopedia, illuminated by exquisite illustrations that depicted each kind of transformation. She turned a few pages and began to read.

The Horne of Power

The Horne of Power can be brandished only by a Witch or Warlock of unusual Strength and Skill. It has but one Limitation: younglings will be unaffected by its hypnotizing song, but this is of little consequence as younglings are usually quite Weak and Unskilled. Any Warlock worthy of the Horne will easily be able to overpower younglings in other ways.

It took Fiona a little longer than usual to make sense of the words, especially since they were written in such elaborate, squiggly letters. But once she did understand them, she had to read it again—just to make sure she was right.

"Darren," she whispered hoarsely. "Look—look at this."

Fiona waited impatiently while Darren puzzled through the difficult text. When he finally looked up from the book, she could tell that he understood too.

"The First Four weren't immune to the horn," Fiona said. "They were just young! That's why it didn't work on them!"

"So a youngling is . . . ," Darren began.

"Here," Fiona said, carefully paging through the ancient book before reading aloud. "'A youngling is but a Changer who has not yet come of age. While even the most juvenile Changers can display some of their powers from birth, the true extent of their skills will not be known until later in life.'"

"Auden Ironbound is on his way, and the First Four think they can still beat him," Darren said. "But—"

"They'll be powerless against the horn now—just like all the other adult Changers," Fiona finished for him.

"Do you think Auden Ironbound knows that?" Darren asked suddenly.

"I have no idea," Fiona replied with a sinking feeling. "This book has been locked away in the rare books room for a long time . . . but it might not be the only copy." She stood up abruptly. "We have to tell Mack and Gabriella, figure out what to do next—"

Just then, Darren's phone buzzed. "My mom's ready to go," he said. "Perfect timing."

"And I'm going to be stuck here for another three hours at least!" Fiona sighed.

"Hey, why don't you come back with us?" Darren asked. "We can get together with Mack and Gabriella and fill them in."

Fiona thought about it for a moment. "I think that should be okay," she said. "Let me text my dad."

> Hey, Dad. I left my math book at school. Darren's mom, Professor Smith, can drive me back to Willow Cove. OK? Sorry! See you at home tonight!

Fiona sent the text, making a silent wish that her father wouldn't be mad at her for missing the poetry reading. At least it wasn't completely a lie—Fiona did leave her math book at school, but only because she'd already finished her homework.

With extra caution, Fiona carefully closed the ancient book and returned it to its glass case. "Let's go," she said, a strange urgency in her voice. "There's no time to lose."

Ninety minutes later, Fiona, Mack, and Darren hunkered down in Darren's old tree house. The rain drummed against the wooden roof that Ray had nailed in place back when Darren was in kindergarten. Darren hardly ever came out to the tree house these days, and it showed—there were dried-up, crunchy leaves scattered across the floor, and more than a few cobwebs. Fiona was glad it was so dim inside. It meant she couldn't see all the spiders that were surely lurking in the corners.

As Fiona glanced at her phone again, Darren asked, "Anything?"

She shook her head. "I'll text her again, but if

Gabriella hasn't responded to my last five messages, I doubt she'll reply to this one."

"What's going on?" asked Mack.

Fiona and Darren took turns telling Mack everything they'd learned about the horn. When they finished, Mack scrunched up his face. "I can't believe this," he said. "Are you telling me that the First Four aren't so special after all? They were just, like, kids?"

"I wouldn't say that," Fiona replied quickly. "The book specifically said that most 'younglings' would be easily overcome. So obviously, they had some kind of unusual strength, even though they hadn't come of age."

"But the reason they were spared from the horn *was* because of their age," Darren pointed out. "We can't count on them to be immune this time."

"Yeah, it *has* been about a thousand years," Mack joked, but nobody laughed.

"So, what are we going to do?" Fiona asked. "We have to figure out the right way to talk to them about it. I can't imagine they'll be happy to hear they're at risk too."

Darren turned to Mack. "You'd better talk to your

grandfather," he said. "I mean, you know him a lot better than the rest of us know Ms. Therian."

"Ah, um, well . . . th-there's just one problem with that," Mack stammered. "Jiichan and I aren't exactly speaking right now."

Fiona's eyes grew wide. "Why not?" she asked. "What happened?"

"We had a stupid fight," Mack admitted. "All because I asked him for a little extra help. I—I—"

"Go on," Darren encouraged him. "You can tell us."

"It's nothing you don't already know," Mack said with a sigh. "I can't transform, okay? I don't even know where to begin. And I *thought* that maybe my own grandfather, who is apparently one of the greatest Changers of all time, could give me some pointers. But I guess that was too much to ask."

While Mack stared at the floor in embarrassment, Darren and Fiona exchanged a glance.

"Mack, you'll figure it out," Fiona finally told him.

"Everybody keeps saying that," Mack replied. "But until it happens, I'm not really a Changer, you know? I'm just some loser along for the ride."

"No way," Darren said firmly.

"Seriously," Fiona agreed. "Don't you think your grandfather and Ms. Therian would *know* if you weren't actually a Changer? They believe in you."

"And we do too," added Darren.

"Thanks, guys," Mack said. But one look at his face told Fiona that Mack wasn't convinced, and the only thing that could change his feelings would be learning how to transform.

"So, you'll talk to your grandfather when you get home?" Darren pressed.

Mack glanced out the tree house window. The rain was falling harder now. "It might be better if we talk to Ms. Therian tomorrow," he suggested.

Fiona frowned. "But—" she began.

"Listen," Mack broke in. "I just had a big fight with my grandfather, right? Now, imagine I walk into the house and tell him he's not quite as powerful as he thinks. That it was all just a misunderstanding. How do you think that will go over?"

"I see your point," said Fiona.

"How about this?" Mack continued. "We'll go to Ms.

Therian tomorrow in Changers class. All of us. Darren and Fiona, since you actually saw the book, you can tell her exactly what it said."

"Can we afford to wait?" asked Darren.

"Yeah. I think so," replied Mack. "Jiichan has had the weather station on all afternoon. The hurricane isn't supposed to hit for three more days."

"*Where* is Gabriella?" Fiona asked suddenly. "I can't believe she hasn't texted me back."

A sudden downpour clattered on the roof, making everyone look up warily. A few minutes later the rain slowed again to a steady patter. It would've been a soothing sound—comforting, even—if there wasn't an evil, power-hungry warlock behind it.

"Maybe she lost her phone," said Darren.

"Maybe," Fiona said.

But everyone could tell she wasn't convinced.

Chapter II
OUT OF TIME

The next morning Gabriella made sure that she was the first one waiting at Lizbeth's locker. Lizbeth's messenger chat last night had made it very clear that anything less would *not* be okay. While she waited, Gabriella sneaked a peek in her little mirror. Ponytail—check. Little gold earrings—check. Normal brown eyes—check. *There is no reason to be worried*, Gabriella reminded herself. Lizbeth was her best friend . . . right?

Suddenly, someone snatched the mirror from Gabriella's hand and snapped it closed. It was Lizbeth, of course.

"You have gotten so vain!" Lizbeth announced. She

was smiling like she was teasing, but her eyes looked like she meant it. "All the time with this mirror, I swear. Just checking to make sure you're still gorgeous, huh?"

"No, it's because my hair is a disaster," Gabriella said automatically. It was always safer to put herself down when Lizbeth acted like this. "I had to redo my ponytail three times already."

"Yeah, it looks pretty frizzy," Lizbeth said smugly. "Must be all this rain."

Gabriella glanced down the hall and waved when she saw Daisy and Katie approaching.

"G!" Daisy exclaimed. "What happened yesterday? Why were you talking with that Mack guy after school? I wanted to hang out."

Gabriella shrugged. "Mack and I just said hi. Then I went home."

"Daisy told me you were tearing it up at practice the other day," Katie said.

"No, whatever." Gabriella tried to laugh it off.

"You were," Daisy insisted, her voice tinged with envy. "I never saw you run so fast or kick so hard. I mean, wow. Even Coach Connors couldn't believe it. I heard him say that the star had gone supernova, what-ever that means."

"I guess Jock Gym for Superjocks is going great for you," Lizbeth remarked.

Gabriella tried to smile but couldn't quite manage it. *Are my nahual powers showing up on the field?* she wondered. If only there was a way to know if her golden eyes had appeared while she ran. *What if I started to transform during practice?* she worried. *Could I stop it? Or would I lose complete control?*

"Hello?" Lizbeth said as she gave a quick tug on Gabriella's ponytail. "Where did you go?"

"Just thinking about my math quiz," Gabriella said. "So, what's up?"

"That's exactly what I wanted to ask you," Lizbeth said, making her blue eyes go all wide. "I have barely seen you since school started. Why are you spend-ing so much time with those weirdos? I mean, Fiona? Seriously? And don't even get me started on the Comic Book King of Willow Cove."

"If Mack was a superhero, he'd be, like, Captain Loser." Daisy giggled. "And Darren is so—"

"No. Darren's okay," Lizbeth cut her off. "He's cute, at least. But you shouldn't be ditching your *best* friends to hang out with him."

"Or anybody else," added Katie.

"I—" Gabriella began, but she stopped herself. Of course she should stick up for her Changer friends; she knew that. But if she did . . .

"Gabriella!"

When Fiona's eager, high-pitched voice echoed off the lockers, Gabriella closed her eyes. *Not now, Fiona,* she thought.

But Fiona was already hurrying over, with Mack and Darren right behind her.

Gabriella didn't need to open her eyes to know that Lizbeth was staring at her. What Gabriella did next would decide everything.

"What do you want?" Gabriella asked coldly.

Fiona paused; blinked. "I— Did you get my texts yesterday?"

Fiona didn't know it, but it was the perfect thing to say.

"Yeah, I got them," Gabriella replied, as if she didn't care. In reality, her phone had accidentally spent the night in her locker at school, but nobody needed to know that.

"Why didn't you respond?" asked Mack.

Gabriella sighed and leaned over to whisper in Lizbeth's ear. Lizbeth loved it. She laughed loudly, even though Gabriella hadn't said anything particularly funny.

Most people would've slunk away by now, but Fiona was determined. "We've got to talk to you," she said, giving Gabriella a meaningful look. "It's urgent."

This time, Katie and Daisy laughed.

"I'm with my *friends*," Gabriella said pointedly. "Why don't you go get some of your own?" she added before turning away, feeling like the worst person in the world. Lizbeth, Katie, and Daisy turned their backs too.

Gabriella tossed her ponytail over her shoulder, like she hadn't noticed the hurt and anger in Fiona's eyes, or the way Darren and Mack had looked at her in disgust. The boys didn't say anything as they left, hurrying after Fiona as she stormed away. Gabriella longed to follow them, to leave Lizbeth behind for good.

But she didn't dare.

For the rest of the day, Gabriella couldn't stop thinking about what a monster she'd been. *I'm as bad as Lizbeth*, she thought miserably. *Worse*. It was unsettling how easy it was to be mean. That's not the kind of person Gabriella wanted to be. She vowed to apologize to Fiona, Mack, and Darren as soon as she got to Changers class after lunch.

Everybody except Ms. Therian was in the gym when Gabriella arrived. She strode across the floor, eager to get the apologizing over with—and to find out what Fiona had wanted to tell her. The three were huddled together by the bench, whispering to one another.

"Hey," she called loudly—a little too loudly, because the echo of her voice off the concrete walls seemed to startle everyone. As Darren spun around, a bolt of lightning shot from his hand and ricocheted off the tile at Gabriella's feet, singeing her shoes.

To Gabriella, the message was crystal clear: they wanted nothing to do with her.

"That was not cool, Darren," she said, her voice trembling. "Not cool!"

Darren pulled himself up to his full height. "Sorry.

It was an accident, and I think you know that," he said. "What's your excuse?"

"What?" Gabriella asked.

"When I hurt somebody, I apologize," Darren said. "You were really hurtful to Fiona this morning—to all of us, actually—but I don't hear any apologies coming from you."

Gabriella's temper flared. "Because you didn't even give me a chance!" she snapped. "I was coming over to talk when you shot a lightning bolt at me!"

"I didn't shoot it *at* you," Darren argued.

Fiona held up her hand. "Forget it, Darren," she said. "It's not worth it."

"Would you *please* give me a chance to explain?" Gabriella begged.

"Explain what?" asked Mack. "It was pretty clear this morning that you care more about being popular than anything else. You know the stakes, you know what's at risk, but your stupid Pony Patrol is more important, I guess."

"Oh, okay, then," Gabriella said. "Maybe we should talk about what's most important to *you*—transforming at all costs. You're way more worried about that than Auden Ironbound. Admit it!"

"Go ahead, rub it in," Mack shot back. "I'm sorry I don't know how to transform. It's not easy for me. It's not like I can just pull on a cloak and *whoosh!* here I am in my Changer form—"

"Hey!" Fiona protested. "I went through a lot to find my cloak, which was *stolen* from me."

"Please. You didn't even know it existed until this week," Mack said.

"What is this, some kind of competition?" Darren demanded. "Maybe if *you* stopped feeling so sorry for yourself, you could figure out how to transform!"

"That's *enough!*"

Everyone had been yelling so loudly that no one had noticed Ms. Therian enter the gym. She shook her head in disgust. "This is what Auden Ironbound wants," she said. "Discord. Allies turning on one another, becoming enemies. Look at you, standing here doing his dirty work for him."

Gabriella knew Ms. Therian was right, but she was too ashamed to say anything. And from the look on everybody else's faces, she wasn't alone.

"We have *work* to do," Ms. Therian continued. "So, if you're all quite finished—"

"Ms. Therian, wait," Fiona spoke up. "There's something we have to tell you. Something urgent."

Ms. Therian fixed her steely gaze on Fiona. "Go ahead."

"Yesterday, Darren and I were at New Brighton University, in the rare books room," Fiona began.

But she never got a chance to finish speaking.

At that moment a loud, low noise filled the gym. The sound of a foghorn, almost, but more terrifying. It resonated through their very bones. Gabriella held herself still. The sound of the horn seemed to suck the air from her lungs. She couldn't breathe. . . .

Then . . . the sweet, empty relief of silence.

"What was—" Darren began to say, his voice shaking.

The sudden flash of light, the scent of smoke . . .

Only Gabriella was truly surprised when Ms. Therian transformed. The werewolf stared at them with unblinking eyes that now glowed an eerie red. *Her eyes*, Gabriella thought, *What happened to her eyes?*

The werewolf flexed; growled a low, menacing sound that was almost worse than the horn. She started to charge for the doors, but Gabriella couldn't let her go. Not like this; not now. The transformation was already upon Gabriella. In her *nahual* form, everything was so much simpler.

With three great bounds Gabriella reached the gym doors before the werewolf. *Ms. Therian, stop!* she commanded. *Where are you going? We need you.*

But Ms. Therian was gone. Gabriella could see that now. The terrifying creature snarled and snapped her sharp fangs at her.

"Move, Gabriella!" Fiona cried. "You have to let her go!"

I can't! Gabriella screamed back in her mind.

The werewolf was so close that Gabriella could feel the heat of breath on her face. Still, she stood her ground, her golden cat eyes unblinking in the face of danger. How long would they have faced off like that, student and teacher, if Darren hadn't intervened?

Gabriella hadn't even seen Darren change, but suddenly, there he was, swooping down on them, creating gale force winds with every beat of his wings. Gabriella fell back from the force, landing on the gym floor with a resounding thud.

When she looked up, the battered gym doors were dangling from their hinges.

Ms. Therian was gone.

Darren, back in his human form, hurried over to Gabriella and held out his hand to help her up. He didn't apologize for knocking her down, and she didn't thank him for saving her life. They both knew those words didn't need to be said.

Fiona approached them then, pale and wide-eyed.

"That loud blast . . . That was the horn of power," she said. "It's happening."

Chapter 12
THE GIFT

Mack's limbs were heavy—stiff, as if his feet had been glued to the floor. It was hard to believe everything he'd seen, but if Mack needed proof, all he had to do was look at the pummeled gym doors.

Jiichan, he thought urgently. *I have to get to Jiichan.*

Mack ran across the room to his friends, but before he could speak, the loudspeaker crackled.

"Attention, teachers and students," Principal Harvey's voice boomed through the gym. "School is dismissed effective immediately due to the hurricane, which has arrived sooner than expected. Students are to report to their buses at once."

In the silence that followed the announcement, no one seemed to know what to do. Then Fiona turned to Mack. "Your grandfather," she began.

Mack swallowed hard. "I never warned him," he said miserably. "He has no idea."

Fiona looked like she wanted to reach for Mack's hand but thought better of it. "He might be okay," she said firmly.

Mack nodded. It was possible. Unlikely, but possible. And that was enough to give Mack hope.

"Go home and find him," Darren said. "Then we'll all meet up at the beach."

"Can somebody *please* tell me what's going on?" Gabriella finally asked. "Ms. Therian . . . What just happened back there? I thought the First Four were immune to the horn."

"I have to go," Mack said abruptly. Let the others fill her in; at this point, all Mack cared about was getting to his grandfather.

The bus ride, normally such an insignificant part of his day, dragged on for what felt like hours. When the bus finally arrived at Mack's house, he bolted off so quickly that he forgot to say good-bye to Joel.

At first everything about home looked normal: Jiichan's car was in the driveway, the front door was locked, and the lights were on. There was even a fresh cup of tea sitting on the kitchen counter.

"Jiichan!" Mack called. "Where are you?"

Silence.

Mack ran from room to room, calling Jiichan's name, but there was no sign of his grandfather. Soon, there was just one place left to look: Jiichan's bedroom. Mack approached it cautiously, with a growing sense of dread. *He's lying down,* Mack told himself. *He didn't expect me home yet. He doesn't even know about the storm.*

As Mack stood in front of the closed door, his hand hovered over the doorknob, hesitating for half a second. Then, mustering his courage, Mack opened the door. He was immediately greeted by a blast of cold, wet air. Jiichan's room was as tidy and orderly as usual . . . except for the shattered plate-glass window overlooking his rock garden. The shredded curtains and deep, fresh scratches on the windowsill told Mack everything he needed to know.

"No!" Mack howled. He backed away, stumbling. It was too much—the shards of glass on the floor, the rain soaking Jiichan's favorite woodblock prints.

It's my fault, Mack thought in despair as he ran to his room. I *should've warned him.* I *should've said something last night, but* I *was stubborn and selfish, too worried about myself . . . and not enough about him.*

And now? What could Mack do now? He couldn't even transform.

Mack kicked open his bedroom door and started pacing back and forth as he tried to figure out what to do next. He'd go to the beach, anyway, even though he wouldn't be much help as a human. However he looked at it, Mack was a failure. I *never should've been in Changers class to begin with,* he thought.

Just then, something on the bed caught Mack's eye: a shiny, lacquered box with an intricate carving on the lid, no bigger than a deck of cards. Mack was certain he'd never seen it before. Inside he found a carefully folded piece of parchment. In his grandfather's perfect hand-writing, the note read:

Mack,

I miss the sound of your voice. My life has
never been so silent since I came to live
with you seven years ago. Silence, though,
can be a gift, for it allows us to hear our
thoughts more clearly. My thoughts center
on how proud I am of you and how proud
your parents would be if they were here.
Like most quarrels, ours is a foolish
one that will soon blow over like an
unexpected storm. Until then, you should
have this. It is your birthright.

Love,

Jiichan

The parchment slipped from Mack's hand as he
blinked hard, trying to rid his eyes of tears. He peeked
into the box, where a sharp object—porcelain? Bone?—
was attached to a leather cord. *What is that?* Mack wondered. He lifted it out of the box and held it high. With
a sudden rush, Mack knew exactly what it was.

A fox tooth.

It was too much: the wind whistling through the shattered window in Jiichan's room, the knowledge that everyone who mattered to Mack was in mortal danger while he was hiding in his bedroom, the glint of the razor-sharp fox tooth. Mack's hands were shaking as he put on the fox tooth necklace, but not from fear or shame.

Rage?

Yes, that was it. Rage . . . frustration . . . and most of all, determination.

Something strange happened to Mack's eyes then, a weird shifting feeling, as though they were stretching. His hands burst into flames, though they didn't burn, and the hair on the back of his neck stood up. No, wait— That wasn't hair at all.

It was fur.

The rest happened all at once, so suddenly that Mack was barely aware of it; an electric charge that ripped through every nerve in his body. His last thought in human form—Is *this*?—was lost to him as the transformation swept his thoughts away.

When it was over, Mack bounded into his *jiichan's* room and caught his reflection in the shattered glass shards on the floor. He was unrecognizable to himself, his reflection strange and surprising: a red fox, sleek and alert, with piercing eyes. The strangest part was how at home Mack felt in this strange skin. All doubts about his destiny as a Changer were gone, now and forever. At last Mack knew exactly what to do—and how to do it.

All of Mack's senses were enhanced now. Things appeared brighter and sharper to his fox eyes, and through the drumming of the rain, he could hear so much more: a car engine half a mile away, a light switched on in the house next door. But what Mack would rely on first was his sense of smell. That, he knew, was the fastest way to find Jiichan. In his human form Mack wouldn't have been able to describe Jiichan's smell, but as a *kitsune*, he could: the smell of green tea and silk screens and patience, of wisdom and bamboo and India ink. That was his *jiichan* . . . and Mack would find him, no matter what.

Mack tracked Jiichan's scent through the broken window, but the trail was fainter outside, mixed with the woodsy scent of trees and the fresh smell of grass. Mack persevered to the edge of the rock garden, where he had his first setback: the trail disappeared in the rain.

Mack shrugged it off. He couldn't afford to get all worked up and disappointed, and he definitely couldn't afford to walk away in defeat. Instead, he started galloping toward the beach as fast as his four strong legs could take him.

They were all there, waiting: the *nahual* and the *impundulu* and the *selkie*, soaked to the skin in the downpour. When they saw Mack in his *kitsune* form, a wild roar arose from them, a sound of celebration like nothing Mack had ever heard before. *Do foxes grin?* he wondered.

This one did.

But only for a second, because Mack—and the others—could feel the danger approaching. Mack got right to the point.

Jiichan's gone, he said. *Just like Ms. Therian.*

And the rest of the First Four, I bet, said Fiona.

Darren spoke next. *What should we do now?*

The plan's ruined, Fiona said. Her dark seal eyes looked even more serious than usual. *We can't count on the First Four. They're part of Auden Ironbound's army now.*

At Mack's frown, Fiona murmured, *Sorry.* But he

could barely hear her. That was his grandfather she was talking about. Mack wouldn't rest until Jiichan was free from Auden's spell.

No, he said, and there was an unexpected growl in his voice. *The plan's not ruined. We are the plan.*

Mack's words hung there as the others stared at him.

We're the First Four now, he continued. *We have to do what they did, a thousand years ago. We have to get the horn and break the spell. There's no one else.*

Mack waited, barely breathing, for one of his friends to respond. If they didn't agree, or if they refused, would he—*could* he—do it on his own?

Then Fiona bowed her head. *By sea,* she pledged.

By sky, Darren said.

Mack and Gabriella exchanged a long look. *By land,* they said at the same time.

So, how are we going to do this? Darren asked.

Mack pointed down the coastline, where the intensity of the hurricane blocked all visibility. *The storm is leaving town,* he said. *We need to catch it.*

Hurricanes have an eye, Fiona spoke up. *Dead center, it's a place of pure stillness and calm.*

You think that's where Auden Ironbound is? asked Mack.

That's where I'd be, she replied.

So, if Auden Ironbound's in the eye of the hurricane . . . , Darren began.

Then the storm surrounding him must be his army of Changers, Mack finished.

We could break them up, Gabriella suggested. You know, distract them. Shatter his defenses.

Divide and conquer, Darren added.

Exactly, Gabriella said. As long as one of us can get the horn . . .

I'll get it, Mack said.

Everyone turned to him.

I have to, he continued. For Jiichan. For everyone.

One by one, the others nodded. Then Gabriella spoke. Wait, she said. I'm sorry . . . about before. The way I acted with Lizbeth. I was awful.

It's— Fiona began.

Please. I have to say this, Gabriella interrupted her. You have to trust me. I'm with you. I'm one of you. And I will never treat you like that again, ever. I promise.

Mack took a deep breath. Okay, he said. Let's do this.

Chapter 13
THE BATTLE

Fiona was the first to depart, diving down through the wildly churning waves. Her promise to her father flickered through her mind for a moment before she remembered her strong flippers and her powerful tail. Fiona the girl had no business going into the storm-tossed ocean. . . . But Fiona the *selkie* was made for this.

The water welcomed her, carrying her over the whitecaps into the depths. But the song that she always heard from the sea was different. Right away, Fiona knew she was not alone. There were others in the ocean, others like her; Fiona could *feel* them, even though the water was so clouded by the surging waves that she couldn't see a thing. And just the way she could feel them, Fiona could also feel that they were part of everything that was happening. Under Auden Ironbound's spell, they were helping the storm rage overhead. It was all connected, Fiona realized; the sea and the sky, the waves and the weather, the tides and the treachery.

I *have to stop the waterborne Changers*, she thought. But *how*? They were Changers like her; they were innocent—caught up in an evil spell. Fiona didn't want to harm them. No, there had to be another way.

Fiona didn't know any *selkie* songs. She couldn't work any magic with her voice yet. But she was fast, and she could distract the Changers, draw them away from the storm.

Fiona darted in and out of the lines, tagging Changer dolphins and seals, circling sea otters and sharks. There was a vacant haze covering their glowing red eyes; Fiona knew Auden had them in his grasp.

As the Changers gave chase, Fiona swam farther out into the ocean, jumping in and out of the waves. One by one, Changers began to surface: seals of all colors;

dolphins, too. She was drawing them out, distracting them from their mission. She realized that the water was starting to calm—it was working!

I'll swim until I pass out, if that's what it takes, Fiona vowed. She breached the water for a deep breath of air and— What was that, over there? The seal with the copper-colored pelt. It was staring at Fiona, but she didn't have time to figure out what it wanted from her.

Fiona dove beneath the waves once more.

Darren was airborne with just two beats of his wings, and in less than a minute, he had flown so far and so high that he could no longer see Mack and Gabriella on the beach below. The wind currents, Darren soon realized, could work with him or against him. He couldn't just fly in a straight line. Instead, Darren had to anticipate each invisible current; where it came from, where it was blowing. Then he had to decide, in a split second, to fly over it, under it, or glide along with it. All the times he'd seen birds in flight, and he'd never once appreciated just how hard it was to fly. Even the clouds were against him, it seemed: dark, dense, and opaque, they obscured just about everything, including the other flying Changers. The higher Darren flew, the darker the sky, until he could barely see anything.

Whoosh!

Darren veered off to the side, nearly missing a collision with some winged creature careening through the growing darkness. His heart was thundering; it wouldn't have been good, he knew, to crash in midair. Darren pictured his wings crumpled, crushed, feathers fluttering through the sky as he plunged to the ground. No, it wouldn't have been good at all.

He still didn't know how, exactly, he was going to help, but one thing was obvious: he needed to *see* if he was going to survive flying through this storm. Just the thought of a midair collision made him so panicked that his talons crackled with anxious sparks.

Sparks.

Of course, Darren thought. *I have lightning on my side.*

He'd never thrown a lightning bolt deliberately, but maybe it was time he tried.

With his wings still beating, Darren turned the rest of his energy to his talons. They were still sparking, and he felt something like an electrical charge building in his neck. The charge gathered strength and intensity and then rolled through his body until—

Crack!

The most brilliant lightning bolt, blue-white with a deep orange aura around it, burst from his talons. It sliced through the clouds, illuminating them and leaving an emptiness in their wake where Darren could see clear down to the beach below.

Darren blinked. That hole in the clouds . . . He wasn't imagining it. Somehow his lightning had actually *broken* the cloud into two.

I *can destroy the storm*, Darren realized. And that was all he needed to send more lightning zinging through the hurricane. Massive bolts whizzed their way through the darkness, leaving streaks of light in their wake. There was still hope.

After Darren and Fiona left, Gabriella felt, suddenly, very small on the vast beach. She was grateful to have Mack with her. It would be easier to face whatever was to come with him by her side.

Let's do it, she said, sounding braver than she felt. Mack nodded, and then they were off, leaving two sets of tracks in the wet sand. Gabriella glanced behind only once, but it was enough to see the smoke unfurling from Mack's paw prints. *So cool*, she marveled before pushing the thought from her mind. Gabriella knew she couldn't afford to get distracted.

After running for several minutes, they were still alone on the beach. With their extreme Changer speed, that didn't make sense to Gabriella. *Where is Auden Ironbound's army?* she wondered as the storm grew more ferocious.

Gabriella cocked her head and listened carefully. There was something under the silence, like the memory of a sound . . . or a vibration . . .

Was it real, or was she just unaccustomed to having supersensitive jaguar hearing? Gabriella wasn't sure. But from the way Mack's fur was standing on end, she had a feeling that he could hear it—or at least sense it—too. And he seemed just as discomfited as she was.

What is *that?* Gabriella finally asked.

I don't like it, replied Mack. *It's creepy.*

Are we in the eye? Gabriella asked suddenly. *I think the rain has slowed down.*

And the wind, Mack added.

Gabriella thought back to what Fiona had said about the eye of the hurricane—*a place of pure stillness and calm*—and thought, *No, that's not what this is. This is something else.*

Near the parking lot, Gabriella could see a mist rolling in. *Wait,* she thought. *That's not right. The mist comes in from the ocean. Not the street.*

She squinted her golden cat eyes and looked harder. Farther. And that's when she realized—

Mack! Gabriella screamed. *Run!*

She shoved the *kitsune* with all her might; he stumbled but understood as he darted on flaming paws toward the true eye of the hurricane, where Gabriella saw the clouds growing darker.

Gabriella, though, stayed rooted to the spot. She knew what was coming, and she stayed, anyway. A stampede of beasts—wolves and bulls and hyenas and jaguars and foxes and snakes—all moving together like some horrible monster, creating a sandstorm as they plowed ahead under the cover of the rain. Gabriella felt strangely calm as she watched them charge toward her.

Pulse pounding, she leapt into the herd of beasts, claws bared. The shattered front line began to chase her, and when she had broken through their ranks she led them as far from Mack as she could. *This is my role*, she thought. *This is the part I play.*

Mack didn't look back. How could he? Either Gabriella would escape or she would be—

No. She would escape. She *had* to escape. Just like Mack *had* to make it to the eye of the hurricane, to get the horn and to . . .

To be honest, Mack wasn't sure *what* he'd do then. He'd have to figure it out when he got there.

Even though he didn't look back, Mack could tell that the horde of Changers was falling farther and farther behind. There was less vibration beneath his paws, and that swirling cloud of sand should have caught up to him by now if they were in pursuit. *Maybe Gabriella is holding them back*, Mack thought. There were other signs, too; hopeful signs. Mack was sure the tide had calmed, and even the clouds seemed less heavy than before. There was a brightness to them, too, as if the sun were trying to shine through.

Then Mack realized he'd reached the eye of the hurricane.

Mack stood very still, his ears pricked up, listening for any sound. Slowly, he turned his head, searching for something, anything, even the slightest movement.

Nothing came.

Show yourself! Mack called.

Mack thought for a moment that maybe the warlock wasn't there after all until he heard a low, guttural laugh in response. Instantly, his fur stood on end, and his lips pulled back in a snarl that showed all his sharp teeth as he prepared to face Auden Ironbound.

You have no power over me! Mack shouted, wondering where those brave words were coming from.

"You mean the *horn* has no power over you," Auden Ironbound corrected him. A thick mist, like a choking fog, began to swirl around Mack's paws. That's when Auden appeared, first in shadow form and then solid. Mack would never be able to say exactly how it happened; if the mist had simply cloaked Auden's arrival, or if he had been right by Mack's side all along, invisible. Either way, there he was: a gaunt, towering figure with a hollow face and empty, emotionless eyes.

"I still have more power than you could begin to comprehend," Auden continued in a lazy drawl. To Mack's astonishment, he almost sounded bored.

Are you going to fight me? asked Mack.

Auden laughed again. "*Fight* you?" he asked. "I don't even know who you *are*. And besides, a mewling pup like you can be easily dealt with."

Auden whistled, as if he were calling a dog, and something bounded out of the shadows. It had nine full tails and familiar white fur that was soft like a snow-drift. The same red flames licked at the creature's paws as Mack's. Mack recognized his grandfather at once, but even if he hadn't, Mack would've known him by scent.

Jiichan! Mack cried in relief. His grandfather was alive, he was safe, he would know what to do. Everything was going to be okay.

But Jiichan's eerie red eyes stared at Mack, as if he were a stranger. Jiichan crouched low, growling savagely, and attacked. Mack was barely able to leap out of the way in time.

Auden laughed in delight. "'Jiichan'?" he crowed. "So, you're the grandson of the great Akira—last of the Kimura *kitsune* line. I'd heard rumors he had a child hidden away. I think I'd very much enjoy watching him tear you to pieces. What do you say? Age versus youth. A fight to the death!"

Under Auden's control, what chance did Mack have of reaching his grandfather? How would he ever be able to break the spell?

The horn, Mack thought.

One thing was certain: Mack couldn't fight Jiichan. Even if he wanted to—and Mack knew already that he never, ever would—Jiichan had to be the most powerful *kitsune* in the world. For more than a thousand years, he'd honed his skills, earning all nine of his tails. Mack had only just transformed for the very first time. He had one tail, which was now dragging in the sand from his fear.

It wasn't a fair fight, not by a long shot, and what made it even worse was that Mack could already see exactly how it would go. As Jiichan circled him, snarling, Mack could only hope that his grandfather would never remember what he was about to do. In that moment Mack had never felt more alone.

No, he thought suddenly. *I'm not alone.* He could feel them—all of them—nearby. Not just Gabriella and Darren and Fiona, but the dozens of other Changers from Auden's army. Strangers to him, but Changers all the same. *This is our fight,* Mack said, reaching out to every Changer on the beach. *Fight with me now.*

Mack called their abilities to him, and they came flowing into his *kitsune* form.

In the end it didn't feel that different from Changing. All Mack had to do was dig down, deep inside himself. He felt his power unfurling, reaching out to the Changers in the sky and on the land and in the sea. Though their bodies were controlled by Auden, their minds, their magic, their spirits were theirs. In an instant, their powers were Mack's powers.

The speed of the jaguar . . .

The strength of the bull . . .

The agility of the dolphin . . .

The cleverness of the seal . . .

The ferocity of the wolf . . .

The wit of the hyena . . .

The bravery of the lightning bird. . .

Suddenly, Mack was the one with powers beyond comprehension. And Auden Ironbound looked like little more than an insect.

The spell will *be broken*, Mack thought, and felt his powers surge.

Even through the fuzzy haze of the horn, Jiichan sensed the change. When Mack roared, Jiichan trembled, hovering on the edge of hypnosis.

As Auden Ironbound observed the way Jiichan cowered, a nasty smile flickered across his face. "I appreciate a fighter," he sneered. "I have no doubt that your demise will be all the more entertaining now. Shall we begin?"

Mack threw his head back and roared again. Then he charged Auden with incredible speed, and the warlock was caught unprepared. He reached for Mack's fur and began to chant a spell, but Mack knocked him over and charged again before Auden had a chance to catch his breath. With the borrowed strength of thousands of Changers coursing through his veins, Mack was too fast, too smart, too brave, too strong for anyone else to triumph over.

Even Auden Ironbound.

Of course, Mack's *kitsune* form didn't just have muscles. It had claws like daggers. Flaming paws. Teeth that could rip and tear. Not even Auden Ironbound's armor, enchanted with the darkest sort of magic, could withstand them. A frenzy of shredding, ripping, and wrecking ensued.

Auden's eyes went wide with fear despite having knocked Mack aside with a magic shield. Mack leaped for him again and caught the warlock's arm with the full force of his jaws. In that moment the horn fell from Auden's jacket, clearly cracked.

The horn, Mack thought.

Mack released the warlock and lunged for the horn.

Then Auden Ironbound disappeared in a gust of smoke. . . .

And everything else did too.

EPILOGUE

The pain came before consciousness; Mack heard himself groaning while his eyes were still shut. Some far-off part of his brain reverberated with a single thought: *Pain means alive.*

Mack opened his eyes. He never would've dreamed that he was back in his own bed, but there he was. How was it possible that everything seemed so . . . *normal*? Was it all just a terrifying nightmare?

Mack's fingers rested on the fox-tooth necklace, which was still hanging around his neck. Not a dream, then, but a reality that was almost too astonishing to comprehend.

Slowly, Mack pulled himself out of bed. Every muscle

ached, even muscles he didn't know he had. He longed to flop back into bed and fall into a deep, dreamless sleep, but he could see the sun was rising outside his window. How long had he been home? And how had he gotten here?

Mack limped to the living room. There was Fiona, wrapped in a thick blanket with a mug of green tea warming her hands. There was Gabriella, who looked almost normal—except for her gleaming gold eyes. And there was Darren, wincing as Ms. Therian bandaged his arm.

And there, by the mah-jongg table, was Jiichan, humming to himself as he set up a game. Mack noticed Sefu and Yara, the other members of the First Four, nearby. The TV was on, but nobody was paying attention to the damage reports from the worst hurricane to make landfall in recorded history.

For a moment, no one noticed Mack.

Then Jiichan looked up. His wrinkled face broke into a wide grin as he held out his arms. "Mack!" he cried.

Everyone started to cheer as Mack bounded across the room, his aches and pains forgotten, to embrace his grandfather. "You're okay," Mack mumbled into Jiichan's shoulder.

"Thanks to you," his grandfather said, "for saving me."

Mack shook his head. He remembered some—most—of what had happened out there on the beach, in the eye of the storm, but so much of it was hazy and unclear.

"How—" he began.

Jiichan's eyes twinkled. "It's an ancient *kitsune* power, very rare," he said. "The ability to borrow strength from another Changer. Of course, I can't think of an occasion when a single *kitsune* borrowed from quite so many different Changers, and all at once."

Mack was a little embarrassed, but Jiichan seemed to understand. "Borrowed strength," he repeated. "They would have fought by your side if they could. Under the spell of the horn, offering you their strength was the most they could do."

"I'm sure you want to know what everyone else was doing while you battled Auden," Ms. Therian spoke up.

"I was in the ocean, surrounded by seals and . . . dolphins?" Fiona said.

"*Encantados*," Yara said. "Like me."

"I don't know any *selkie* magic yet, but I drew the waterborne Changers away from the storm. And it was so weird, but . . . the waves quieted. It was like the distraction stopped the Changers from concentrating on making the storm."

"I was flying through the storm," Darren remembered. "It was so dark up there. I couldn't see a thing. So I started throwing lightning bolts, and they cut through the clouds like knives."

"I remember that!" Mack said suddenly. "I thought it was the sun."

"I've never known such a young *impundulu* to be capable of creating so much lightning," Sefu said from across the room. "You nearly struck me while I was in my *bultungin* form, as a hyena, running at this brave young woman." He gestured to Gabriella.

Mack turned to Gabriella too. "I didn't want to leave you," he said.

"You had no choice," she replied quickly. "It was fine—I was fine. I started running, and they chased after me. Just the way I wanted them to—away from you."

"That was so brave. And also really cool," Mack said, a note of admiration in his voice.

Gabriella waved away the compliment. "Not as brave

as destroying Auden Ironbound," she said. "You cracked the horn and broke his spell on the Changers. Ms. Therian says they've all gone home. Well, most of them."

"Some stayed to help with the cleanup," Darren said. "Luckily there's no sign of Auden, though."

Mack swallowed hard. "So Auden Ironbound is . . . ?" he asked.

Jiichan and Ms. Therian exchanged a long look. "He escaped," Jiichan said. "I don't . . . None of us can figure out how he managed it."

"Dark magic, no doubt," muttered Yara.

"But he escaped, and he took the damaged horn with him," Jiichan continued.

Mack's face was troubled. So it was all for—for what? Auden Ironbound was still out there. The horn was still out there. Mack had delayed the inevitable, maybe, but for how long?

"Auden Ironbound is but a shell of what he was," Jiichan said, as though he could read Mack's thoughts. "And the horn is cracked. I expect it will take a long while for him to repair it. More than enough time to prepare for what comes next."

"We won't soon forget what you did for us," said Ms. Therian, looking at each of her four students. "In the darkest hour, all of you rose to the occasion. That's no small thing."

"We should know," Yara joked. The First Four laughed harder than anyone.

Jiichan stared at Mack with a strange expression on his face. "I think you should transform," he said.

"Here?" Mack asked. "Now?"

Jiichan nodded. "See what your bravery has earned you," he replied.

Mack tried not to feel self-conscious as he transformed, right there in the middle of the room. He glanced around at all the faces looking at him. Everyone seemed so happy . . . so *proud* . . .

Then Mack turned around, and to his astonishment, he saw that he had a second tail. Just like that, it had appeared—strange and beautiful and unexpected.

"A *kitsune* earns a new tail with each ability learned," Jiichan said in a low voice. "This is why I cannot help you, much as I would like to. Who can say what powers live within you? Only time will reveal them. Time, and your own dedication. There can be great danger in teaching certain *kitsune* abilities before a student is ready—and even greater danger in forcing that first transformation. It is a mistake that . . . that I will not make again."

Mack didn't know what to say.

"Besides, you don't need my help, Mack," Jiichan continued. "You're going to figure things out just fine on your own."

Mack transformed back into his human form so that he could hug his grandfather again. "Please," he whispered, "call me Makoto."

There was no reason, Mack realized, why he couldn't be Makoto to his grandfather and Mack to his friends. If he could be both human and Changer, boy and *kitsune*, well, then, *anything* was possible. Mack was aware of a fundamental truth: now more than ever, it was crucial to embrace all the possibilities, all the opportunities, all the parts of himself.

Mack transformed for the third time, just because he could. It was getting easier and easier, giving him the confidence and learning that as long as he worked hard—as long as he tried with all his might—nothing was beyond his grasp. One by one, Fiona, Darren, and Gabriella transformed, too, under the watchful eyes of the First Four.

After all, Auden Ironbound would return.

And when he did, all the Changers would be ready.

What challenge will the Changers face next?

Here is a sneak peek at

THE HIDDEN WORLD OF
Changers

The Emerald Mask!

Run.

It was the only thought on Gabriella Rivera's mind; the thought that played again and again, over and over, as she darted down the soccer field.

Run.

Somewhere, deep down, Gabriella was probably aware of the world beyond the field: the golden autumn sun slicing through a clear, blue sky; the cheerleaders practicing a new routine on the track; the late buses rumbling in the parking lot, waiting to take everyone home from their after-school activities. But in the moment, all Gabriella cared about was:

The goal at the end of the field.

The tattered practice ball at the tip of her foot.

And the pounding of her heart, strong and steady, as she ran at top speed.

Run.

Other players? What other players? Gabriella had left them all in the dust—except for Trisha, who was practicing her goalie skills across the field. A sudden alertness washed over Gabriella as she fixed her eyes on Trisha. Trisha was poised, ready to block any goal Gabriella tried to make. It was totally obvious that Trisha was trying to predict Gabriella's next move. Gabriella could tell from the way Trisha's shoulders were tensed; from the way her eyes followed Gabriella, watching for a sign, a tell . . .

No way, T, Gabriella thought. *Not this time.*

An extra burst of speed—Gabriella didn't know exactly how she channeled it, but she had a pretty good idea . . .

The thud of her foot making contact with the ball—

Her toes reverberating inside her cleat—

The solid leather ball sailed through the air as free and weightless as the fluff from a dandelion.

I *did that,* Gabriella marveled. I *did it.*

What choice did Trisha have but to drop to the ground, face-first in the grass? Better than a soccer ball to the face, there was no doubt about that.

Time shifted, somehow, and the seconds between

the ball tearing through the net and the piercing shriek of Coach Connors's whistle slowed, stretched while Trisha lifted her head and locked eyes with Gabriella.

Something in Trisha's eyes made Gabriella flinch, and the spell was broken. Sound came rushing back: the whistle, the cheers from the rest of their teammates, the voices of kids heading to their buses. All the ordinary noises one would expect to hear at Willow Cove Middle School on a Tuesday afternoon.

"Great work, girls. Excellent practice," Coach Connors was saying. "You play like that on Saturday and the Middletown Marauders don't stand a chance."

Trisha was already lifting herself out of the dirt, but Gabriella reached for her arm, anyway.

"Trisha, I am so sorry," Gabriella said as she helped Trisha to her feet. "Are you okay?"

"Sorry? Are you serious?" Trisha asked, ignoring Gabriella's question. "What you did—that move—it was *incredible*! I've been playing goalie for years, and I have *never* seen anyone score like that. *Ever.* Coach is right. If you play even half that good on Saturday, we're going to win for sure."

Coach Connors approached them with the ball bag.

"Blew another net, Coach," Trisha reported.

Coach Connors shook his head as he examined the ragged hole where the ball had blasted right through the net. "I can't get mad," he said. "We've never had so many consecutive wins before. The team is on fire this year. But, Gabriella, *try* to take it a little easy on the equipment, would you?"

"Sorry, Coach," Gabriella said. "I got a little carried away."

"I know," Coach Connors replied. "But save it for Saturday, okay?"

Then he tossed the ball bag toward Trisha; as team captain it was her responsibility to gather all the soccer balls that had been used for drills.

"Here," Gabriella said, reaching for the bag. "Let me help."

"Thanks," Trisha replied. They split up for a while, crisscrossing the field as they gathered several soccer balls. Soon there was just one ball left—the one that Gabriella had kicked through the net. Only hitting the side of the school had stopped it.

"You go," Gabriella said to Trisha. "I know you have a bus to catch. I walk home, so I'm not in a rush."

Trisha glanced over her shoulder at the buses idling in the parking lot. "This is my responsibility," she began.

"And it's my fault the ball is all the way over there," Gabriella said, laughing easily in the sunshine. It felt good—*so good*—to be at the top of her game, to be unstoppable on the field, to have such good friends playing by her side. She couldn't *wait* for Saturday's game.

Then Gabriella noticed she was laughing alone.

"What?" she asked self-consciously as Trisha stared at her. "Is there grass in my hair or something?"

"It's just . . . Your eyes . . . They're brown, right?" Trisha asked, peering at Gabriella. "They look brown now, I mean. But on the field . . ."

Gabriella fought the urge to look down; to cover her eyes and sprint away from Trisha. *Act normal,* she ordered herself, which was easier said than done.

"I thought they were yellow!" Trisha continued, totally oblivious to Gabriella's discomfort. "Like a cat or something! Isn't that weird?"